KINDRED HEARTS

After a humiliating break-up, Kate decides to spend Christmas alone in a secluded countryside cottage. But her plans for solitude evaporate when she meets the guest at the neighbouring cottage — exciting, unpredictable Alex. As Kate continues to bump into Alex in unexpected places, her oldest and best friend Chris warns her off her new acquaintance. She is furious — who is he to interfere? But as she realises that Alex might not be what she is searching for, Kate wonders if she's been looking for love in all the wrong places . . .

WENDY KREMER

KINDRED HEARTS

Complete and Unabridged

LINFORD
Leicester

First published in Great Britain in 2017

First Linford Edition
published 2019

A catalogue record for this book is available
from the British Library.

ISBN 978–1–4448–4327–9

Published by
F. A. Thorpe (Publishing)
Anstey, Leicestershire

Set by Words & Graphics Ltd.
Anstey, Leicestershire
Printed and bound in Great Britain by
T. J. International Ltd., Padstow, Cornwall

This book is printed on acid-free paper

Best-laid Plans

It was Christmas Eve.

Yesterday had been hectic at the shop, with last-minute shoppers hoping to find something special. Kate had even managed to sell a mid-Victorian Davenport, and Derek had promised to deliver it this morning.

With a heightened sense of freedom, she watched small swirling speckles of white descending as the train travelled into the countryside. Large snowflakes soon replaced the specks, and it began to blanket the ground. Daydreaming, she stared at her reflection in the window and hoped the snow would last. Despite everything, snow would make this Christmas special.

Her parting from James had been unexpected and embarrassing. She wondered if she was to blame in some way, but her friends Gail, and later Chris, insisted she wasn't.

Gail was joining some friends in France for Christmas and, as the train sped on, Kate recalled their conversation a few days ago, when she'd told Gail that she and James had finished. Kate expected Gail to find excuses for him because Gail and James were both high-flyers with well-paid jobs. They also held similar professional beliefs and had the same attitude about many other things. There was one big difference, though — Gail was loyal, and her friendship never wavered.

'James was never right for you,' Gail had told her. 'You were fundamentally opposites in so many ways. I picked up nasty rumours about him a while back, and if we were ever out together, I couldn't help but notice he was a compulsive flirt. Not the best recommendation for a trustworthy boyfriend.'

'So why didn't you warn me?'

Gail reached out and tapped the back of her hand.

'You wouldn't have believed me, and

it was none of my business. I'm not sorry. I'm sure you'll be better off without him. Are you very miserable?'

Kate had shook her head.

'Funnily enough, no, I'm not. I realise now that there were always things about James I didn't like. I ignored my misgivings and thought things would improve.'

'Weren't you spending Christmas with his family?'

Kate nodded.

'I haven't told Mum and Dad that we've broken up yet. I expect they're reckoning on wedding bells. I've decided to go away for a couple of days on my own.'

'What? Over Christmas? Where are you going?'

'I've rented a cottage in the country. I'm looking forward to it.'

'You're bonkers, but in a way I do understand. If I wasn't going away, I'd come with you.'

Kate had met Chris the next day. He was walking down the street and told her he was on his way to a business meeting in London.

She admired how Chris always looked up to the mark. In casual clothing, he could have advertised any kind of sportswear or male cosmetics. He looked just as good in business wear. This morning he wore a dark blue business suit, a sparkling white shirt, and a narrow striped tie. The folds of his soft overcoat moved in the wind. They'd been friends since school days and kept nothing back from each other.

He smiled when they met.

'Hi! I'm catching the ten thirty train, so I can't stop. Will I see you again before Christmas? You're going away with James, aren't you?'

'I was, but I'm not any more. We're finished.' She wrapped her coat a little tighter and waited for his reaction.

He was silent for a moment as he looked at her. When he spoke, his voice was firm.

'Good riddance! He wasn't right for you.'

'Why does everyone keep saying that? Gail told me that yesterday.'

'Did she? She was right. So you'll be going home for Christmas?'

'No, I've rented a cottage in the country, and I'm looking forward to it.'

'Why on earth are you doing that?' he said with a significant lifting of his brows.

'Because everyone at home will want to sympathise and commiserate. Aunt Sally will be there on Christmas Day. Her fiancé jilted her on her wedding day. Can you imagine it?'

He laughed softly and his eyes twinkled.

'Would you like me to come with you?'

'No. You've promised to visit your mum and dad. Don't disappoint them. But thanks for offering.'

He checked his watch.

'Must go! You take care of yourself. Tell me all about it when you get back.'

* * *

Kate realised suddenly that her train was drawing into the station. She'd reached her destination. Some people began collecting their things and getting ready to descend.

Fluffy snow lay on the ground, and her boots made clear imprints as she left the station. In the station forecourt, she looked up at a pewter coloured sky. It heralded that there was more snow on its way.

She hoped to find a taxi stand, but she was disappointed. It wasn't a big town. She asked someone hurrying along the pavement if there was a car-hire or taxi company in the town. The woman, laden with Christmas shopping, gave her hurried directions.

Kate found the offices mid-way down the main street. The shops were aglow with Christmas lights and decorations. People were bustling around, busy with their final preparations.

Bursts of icy wind blew in her face before she reached the office and pushed the door open. The middle-aged woman behind the desk looked up.

Tugging her suitcase behind her, Kate shook the snow from her scarf.

'I need a taxi for a trip to the outskirts of the town. According to my information it's a place about three miles from here.'

The woman shrugged.

'We only have three taxis and they're all out.' She glanced at the wall clock. 'They are on their last trips. The weather forecast is bad for the rest of today and tomorrow. There's a storm warning, and our boss has told us all to go home early. From now until after Boxing Day we only accept emergency calls. The boss will handle that himself. I was just about to close and go home.'

Kate's heart sank.

'Oh, no!' She glanced out of the window. 'Even if the weather was good, three miles is a long way, and I don't know where it is! Is there another company I can try?'

The woman shook her head.

Reading the disappointment and

seeing the growing desperation on Kate's face, she raised her eyebrows.

'Where are you going? Perhaps I can suggest something?'

'It's called Honeysuckle Cottage, Broadacres Lane.'

The woman's expression mellowed and she gave Kate a slow smile.

'You may be in luck. Bill is still out with his final passenger, but he might be able to take you. Broadacres Lane is on his way home. I'll just check.'

Kate crossed her fingers and watched as the woman went into the back room. She hadn't reckoned with a problem of getting from the town to the cottage.

She heard a brief conversation and the crackle of a radio connection.

When she returned, the woman's face broke into a friendly smile.

'Bill will take you. He reckons he'll be here in about twenty-five minutes.'

Kate felt tangible relief.

'That's fantastic! I'm so grateful.' She glanced at her watch. 'I've time to shop for a few things.'

The woman sounded amused.

'Rather you than me. I did my last-minute shopping first thing this morning and it was already packed. Don't be late! If Bill gets ratty he may not wait.'

Kate nodded. She'd be back in time. She didn't need to buy much. She'd arranged for the owners to leave some groceries at the cottage, and she could manage easily without too many last-minute additions.

The wind was at her back and her long coat flapped about her boots as she headed for a nearby small supermarket. The snow looked like icing sugar where it hadn't been disturbed by blustery squalls or passing feet.

She checked her watch frequently as she stood in line at the checkout and began to wonder if spending Christmas in the country was a good idea after all.

With her backpack bulging, she returned to her waiting suitcase in the office. There was a man talking heatedly to the woman behind the desk. He wore a heavy dark jacket and a dark woollen cap and a thick scarf concealed most of his face.

Kate moved to the window alcove. She shook her long scarf free of snow and pulled her woollen cap even tighter over her ears. She was glad that her knee-length boots had artificial fur lining. Her feet were deliciously warm.

Feeling much happier, Kate was looking forward to spending Christmas on her own after all. She looked forward to lazing, watching TV, reading books, and catching up on sleep. Her plans had been different a couple of weeks ago, but then she'd found James with someone else when she'd called unexpectedly at his flat — and they hadn't been sharing a cup of tea.

She still recalled how humiliated and cheated she'd felt. Then she had spotted the advert for the cottage in a magazine and thought it was the solution. She was reluctant to celebrate at home and have to explain why she wasn't with James.

The weak sun was low on the horizon and daylight had faded completely. She glanced out of the window down the road. Bathed in the soft light from the overhanging lamp-posts, the street was still full of busy shoppers and a group of carol singers were braving the elements in front of the local pub.

Clusters of last-minute customers looked tired and frustrated as they buried their faces in their scarves and defied the elements. Kate saw a taxi approaching, its windscreen wipers working frantically to keep pace with the falling snowflakes.

The woman behind the desk was busy, so Kate just called across.

'The taxi's here. Happy Christmas — and thank you!' Kate dragged her suitcase out on to the pavement and the wind whipped at her scarf.

The taxi driver got out, smiled, and opened the boot with a flourish.

'You must be the young lady who wants to get to Honeysuckle Cottage. Gloria explained everything. Load your stuff. I won't be a jiffy. I'll just clear things with Gloria first.'

Kate shoved her suitcase and rucksack into the boot and got in.

Bill brought someone with him — the man in the dark anorak. He opened the door and leaned towards her.

'Apparently, we're going in the same direction so I hope you won't mind if we share the taxi. There isn't another one.'

She wanted to reach the cottage without any more complications, and now this man was messing things up. Her cheeks grew warm. She tried to be reasonable.

Fidgeting with her cap, she turned to him.

'Are you sure there's no alternative?'

He gave her a pained stare.

'Certain. All the other drivers have gone home. The snow has added to the general chaos and there's no other possibility — apart from borrowing Santa's sleigh, and it's not free till tomorrow. If it was decent weather and I knew where to go, I'd walk. In this snow, it's hard to recognise anything and I'm a stranger to the district.'

Bill nodded.

'That's true, lad. All fields look alike when covered in snow. Local road signs are few and far between and you'll get lost. I'm looking forward to getting home to my wife and a blazing fire, too. So let's get going.'

Kate cleared her throat and concentrated on her travelling companion's face. It was attractive and he had large dark eyes. Snowflakes rested on his long eyelashes and she noted that he needed a shave. She reminded herself it was the season of goodwill.

'Where are you going?'

'A place called Honeysuckle Cottage,' he told her. Snowflakes were beginning to cover his cap.

'That can't be right!' Kate snapped. 'I've booked Honeysuckle Cottage! It's mine for the next week.'

He gave a disbelieving shake of his head.

'No, it isn't! I've rented it.'

'It's mine!' she insisted, feeling slightly overwhelmed. 'I'm sorry, but you'll have to find a hotel and get your money back after Christmas.'

His expression was stony.

'I booked, I paid, and I have written confirmation. Honeysuckle Cottage is mine until the thirtieth of December. Just because you got into the taxi first doesn't mean you have special rights.'

An Uneasy Truce

'If you were a gentleman, you'd waive your rights!' Kate snapped back, feeling maddened.

He looked up at the sky and tugged at his scarf.

'I'm not worried if you think I'm not a gentleman. I don't intend to waive my rights. I need the cottage for a few days.' He paused and studied her face. 'Look, there's a mix-up, and it's too late to contact the owner now. I'm prepared to make concessions. We can share.'

Kate stared at him in amazement.

'Are you suggesting I spend the holidays with a complete stranger just because the owner has muddled things up?'

He shrugged.

'It's either that or nothing. Please yourself.'

Kate was dazed. He was so rude! She

didn't want to share. If he refused to budge and the town didn't have a hotel, she might end up spending Christmas Eve in the station waiting room. She wouldn't phone her dad for help in this weather. She didn't want to give in, and wouldn't.

'I can't imagine being in the same room as you for longer than five minutes, never mind sharing a cottage for a week!'

His eyes twinkled briefly.

'Make up your mind. We're holding Bill up.' He looked up briefly at the swirling snowflakes. 'Perhaps we can split the place somehow and avoid each other. There are two bedrooms — I can remember reading that in the brochure. It's up to you, but I'm going to Honeysuckle Cottage with or without you.'

Kate's colour increased. What an offensive man. The station waiting room seemed infinitely more appealing than time spent with him. Perhaps the pub had a room. She began to slide across the seat.

Bill broke in.

'Before both of you bring out the artillery, I happen to know there are two sides to Honeysuckle Cottage. It used to be an old smithy and a cottage and it's now two holiday homes. I've taken visitors there before. In summer, of course — not many people would choose to stay in such an isolated spot in the middle of winter.'

Kate looked at him wide-eyed. She repeated. 'There are two cottages, with their own entrances?'

Bill nodded and turned to the stranger.

'Why don't you put your stuff in the back and get in, young fellow? I want to get home before my car gets stuck in a snowdrift.'

The man loaded his backpack and suitcase and got into the passenger seat next to Bill. He ignored Kate and she him.

Satisfied that everyone was finally ready, Bill set off. During the journey, the two men discussed various football teams and their position in the league.

It looked as though she had a cottage to herself after all. She wasn't likely to see much of him once they were there, especially not in this weather. She stared at the back of his woollen cap and hoped he wasn't a serial killer or some kind of psychopath.

When they reached the outskirts, the snow covered everything in a thick layer. The wind was piling drifts against the high hedging on both sides of the road, and the verges were under the snow. Bill drove in the middle and they didn't meet any other vehicle.

Kate only saw far-off lights flickering in the darkness through farmyard gates in the hedges. She reminded herself that it was what she'd wanted — no parties, no other people, and isolation for a whole week.

They travelled for about 20 minutes then Bill braked slowly. He pointed towards a side road.

'That's the sloping lane that leads down to the cottages. I'll drop you off here, if I may. If I drive down there, I won't be able to get back up without help. It's a steep incline.'

Both passengers scrambled out, regained their possessions, and both spoke at once.

'How much do we owe you?'

Bill told them and they split the amount, each adding a generous tip. They wished Bill a merry Christmas and waited as his taxi wheels spun for a second or two before he moved off again. Soon the taxi's red tail-lights disappeared from sight.

Kate shoved her purse back into her rucksack. She and the man ignored each other and moved wordlessly towards the side lane.

The snow was halfway up her boots, and dragging her suitcase through the snow wasn't much fun. She was glad her boots were solid and sensible.

As she struggled along, she recalled Gail's favourite boots. They were bright red, high-heeled, very striking, and totally unfitting for conditions like these.

The man forged ahead. Kate felt a

little uncomfortable about how she'd handled the situation. It wasn't his fault or hers. He'd been prepared to compromise, but she hadn't.

She used the track left by his suitcase to make it a little easier for herself. Dragging hers was more difficult than she'd expected. Her breath misted on the cold air, and her case kept wobbling off course.

Thorn hedging bordered the lane. If she hadn't been hurrying to get to the cottage, Kate would have enjoyed the way the snow conjured up a lace-like impression between the twigs and branches.

The man lifted his suitcase above his head, and made faster progress.

Kate spotted the roof and chimneys of a long building below them. She wasn't strong enough to shoulder her own case, so she continued to drag it along. She paused to catch her breath and adjust her scarf. Snowflakes fell on a silent landscape. The man disappeared around a gentle bend in the lane and she set off again.

For a while she made good progress, but then the lane banked and was very slippery underfoot. She wondered if there was a natural spring somewhere in the banking. Trying to be careful while pulling a defiant suitcase, and with a bulky pack on her back, one foot slipped and the rest followed. She landed on her backside, slid into a drift on the side of the lane, and parted company with her case on the way. Trying to struggle to her feet, she consoled herself with the knowledge it wasn't far to the cottage now.

She heard him laughing gently as he came striding back up the road. He stopped in front of her and held out his hand. He looked like a dark giant with snowflakes scurrying and floating around him in the sparse lighting.

She ignored his hand and scrambled awkwardly to her feet. She brushed herself down, and stared at him defiantly.

'I'm perfectly all right, thank you!'

He chuckled in the darkness.

'I can see that. Are you really OK?'

She nodded. She wanted to ignore him, but found herself drawn to his dark eyes twinkling in the darkness and the white of his smile.

'I've dumped my stuff and checked my booking,' he said. 'I have side A you have B. I was just closing my door when I heard you yell.'

'Did I yell?' she replied, biting her lip. 'I can't remember.' Kate noted that layers of snow were building a shape like a Christmas tree on his cap. It reminded her of her mother's Christmas cake decorations. She pulled herself together so as not to chuckle. 'I'm fine.'

'Oh, don't be so obstinate. Go ahead. I'll grab your case.' He waved his gloved hand and indicated towards her soaked jeans. 'You should get out of those fast or you'll spend Christmas in bed with a cold.'

Trying to sound unconcerned, she gave in. She did feel uncomfortable and very wet.

'It wasn't my intention to land on my backside in the snow.'

He chuckled and she liked the sound.

'I can imagine!'

Her voice wavered.

'Well . . . if you don't mind. Thank you.' She moved on carefully towards the cottages and he went back to retrieve her suitcase. There was a light coming from a window on the left-hand side. She hurried along the fence to the other side. Snow had accumulated in piles everywhere and she struggled to open the gate.

The pathway to the porch was only discernible because here and there tips of greenery showed along its edges. When she reached the porch, she fumbled to find the key where the owner said he'd leave it — under the mat. It was ice-cold. She fitted it into the lock and opened the door.

She'd arrived! Dumping her ruck-sack, she fumbled in the darkness for the light switch. She pulled off her cap and went back to the doorway. The man was already coming up the pathway with her case above his head. He set it down inside the door.

'There! Let's hope we can get out of this place after Christmas. Do you know what the long-term forecast is like?'

Kate was glad to have arrived; she hadn't given a thought to leaving. She tried to sound friendly.

'No, but the lady in the taxi office said something about a storm warning and more snow.' She looked up at the flakes of white thistledown still floating down thick and fast. 'It can't last; it never does. In fact, it's years since we had a white Christmas. I expect it will have disappeared by tomorrow morning.'

'I don't think so; it's too cold to melt away overnight.' He removed a hand from his glove and held it in her direction.

'By the way, my name is Alex — Alex Corbett.'

Kate took it automatically and found

it was warm and pleasing.

'And I'm Kate — Kate Fellows. I'm sorry I was so grumpy, I was looking forward to a solitary Christmas, and I thought you might torpedo it.'

'Water under the bridge.' He smiled. 'I wasn't at my best, either. We both want peace and quiet. Merry Christmas!' He turned away.

'Thanks for fetching my suitcase. Have a good Christmas!'

He pushed his hand back into his glove and waved it above his head.

'Will do!'

She watched him stroll back along the fence to his cottage, then closed and locked the door.

She explored the cottage. The owner had laid a fire in the fireplace and she put a match to it. The kindling was dry and it caught immediately. Soon the bigger logs were crackling and flames warmed the surroundings. She stood watching the flames for a moment.

The cottage also had gas central heating. She had to find out first how to switch it on. There were instruction manuals piled on the table with a note of welcome and a bottle of wine from the owner.

She drew the heavy curtains and hung up her coat before she slipped out of her boots and wet clothes. Unzipping her suitcase, she quickly found leisure trousers, thick socks and slippers.

She felt better and the fire was beginning to take the chill out the air. Piling on a few more logs from a basket on the side, a faint smell of apple filled the air as the flames devoured the wood.

She sighed contentedly. It looked as though things were going to be first-rate after all.

She looked through the manuals for instructions on the gas stove, opened the gas bottle in the adjoining cupboard, then put the kettle on to boil. The groceries she'd asked the owner to get were on the table or in the fridge.

The knowledge that she was alone was strange, but not scary. She was miles from anywhere, in the depth of a snow-covered countryside and looking forward to a couple of days of enjoying herself and forgetting James.

Alex Corbett was next door, but he wanted to be alone, too, so that was no problem. In fact, his presence was a comfort. Being alone in this deserted cottage for a week might have been more challenging than she'd expected.

The kettle whistled and she made herself a cup of coffee. She emptied her backpack and found the mince-pies were squashed, but that didn't matter; no-one else would see them. She bit into one and found it was quite delicious.

Kate flipped through the various manuals about the DVD player, TV, the central heating, and the oven. She noted the rich supply of paperbacks on a shelf.

She figured out how to start the gas central heating quite easily, and the radiators began to send warmth through-out all the rooms. Then she climbed the narrow staircase to the first floor and chose the larger bedroom of the two. It had a low ceiling, and sloping walls.

It was heaven to have a hot shower and slip into some flannel pyjamas. Looking out of the bedroom window set into the thick walls, she thought she could hear church bells ringing somewhere in the distance.

Was it her imagination — or was the sound really carried here on the wings of the wind?

Once she'd secured the dying fire for the night, she put out the lights, went upstairs and picked up the novel she'd started a couple of days previously.

She slipped under the duvet and soon felt warm and cosy.

Supported by multiple pillows, she read for a while, before she finally put the book aside and settled down for the night.

A Helping Hand

It was magical to wake up to a thick layer of snow on the window-sill. It had stopped snowing, and defiant trees with skeleton-like branches were scattered between majestic evergreen and thorn hedging along the edges of fields spreading into the distance.

An ivory-coloured faux fur blanket covered her bed and gave the room a luxurious feeling. She touched the radiator. It was warm. She'd left all the radiators on during the night, deciding the cottage was mostly unoccupied at this time of year and the walls needed extra heating. She opened the window and cold fresh air flooded the room.

Kate dithered between making herself a cup of tea and getting back into bed. The bed won. Lying in comfort, she heard someone moving around next door. She looked up at the slanting ceiling. It was Christmas Day and she hoped James was having a miserable time.

Kate dozed for a while, but finally hunger took her downstairs to prepare some coffee and toast. Switching on the radio, Christmas carols filled the air as she filled the kettle. She thought briefly about her parents. Her mother would be busy in the kitchen. Her sister and family were coming for Christmas dinner.

Her parents were disappointed when she'd told them she was spending Christmas with James and his family in Scotland. That was all before she'd broken up with him. She hadn't corrected the illusion when she rang them two days ago. She hoped they'd understand when she told them why she'd opted to spend Christmas alone.

After breakfast, and deciding what she was eating for her Christmas dinner, she got dressed and cleared the debris out of the fireplace. She re-laid the fire and decided to forage in the garden for some holly if she could find some. Even though she was alone, it didn't mean she wasn't going to celebrate.

Slipping into her boots and warm coat, she pulled on her woolly hat and wrapped her scarf tightly round her neck, then ventured out into the snowy fields at the back of the house.

The sun was very low and its weak rays reflected and sparkled on the surface like diamonds as she struggled towards a holly tree in the corner of a neighbouring field. She looked back when sounds coming from the cottages caught her attention.

Alex was gathering logs from a pile against the walls. He saw her and lifted a free hand. Kate waved back and was glad he'd forgotten yesterday's clash.

The freshness of the air was invigorating. She wrestled with a holly tree for some thin branches using the kitchen scissors, and cut some fir from another tree. She looked forward to a mug of steaming hot chocolate, then she would decorate the cottage with her greenery.

On her way back, she somehow slipped and lost her balance, and searing pain shot through her ankle. She struggled to her feet and found it was impossible to put any weight on that foot. She gritted her teeth.

'I don't believe this! Why me?'

Alex was still picking up wood. He must have seen what had happened. He let the logs fall and came across. He picked up the scissors.

'You're lucky you didn't land on top of these. What on earth are you doing?'

Feeling rather stupid as she stood facing him on one leg, Kate wished she could think of a rational answer that didn't sound idiotic.

'I was collecting holly and I slipped.'

'What do you need holly for?'

'Why does anyone need holly at this time of the year?' she replied, trying to sound blasé. 'It's always been part of our family's Christmas decorations.'

'Holly doesn't last five minutes indoors in today's central heating. Are you expecting your family?'

She shook her head.

'Then you picked it just for yourself?'

She nodded.

He shook his head.

'Apart from the fact that I don't understand why you bothered, do you realise that holly trees are a protected species? You are breaking the law.'

Looking more submissive, she nodded.

'I know. You're right, but it's too late now. And I only took a couple of small branches, honestly!'

For a couple of seconds, they regarded each other silently, then he raised an eyebrow.

'Since you are standing on one leg like a flamingo, I presume you have hurt yourself?'

The wind was kissing the surface of the snow, and blowing gusts of cold breezes across the fields towards them. Kate hoped he would shut up soon. She was growing colder by the minute.

'I hurt my foot, but it's nothing serious. I'll be all right soon.'

He couldn't quite hide the amusement on his face as he watched her. His dark eyes twinkled and the wind was playing havoc with his thick wavy hair.

'You seem to attract trouble, don't you?'

Kate wished he would go away.

'I'm all right. I'll hop back and be inside in no time at all. Please carry on with whatever you were doing.'

He ignored her remark.

'Don't be so optimistic. If you're standing on one leg, it means it hurts. You are quite likely to slip again before you reach the back door. Put your arm around my neck and start hopping!'

She considered refusing, but he was right. Trying to get back without accepting his support would be silly and look undignified. She might slip again, and her foot did hurt — she couldn't pretend it didn't.

She looked regretfully at the discarded fir and holly lying where they'd landed. She didn't have enough courage, or cheek, to mention it.

To her silent satisfaction, he bent and picked it up.

Holding the bunch in one hand, together with the kitchen scissors, he looked at her elevated foot.

'Can you wiggle your toes?' he asked. 'If you can, maybe you haven't broken anything, but you should get out of that boot fast. If your foot swells, you'll be in real trouble.'

Kate tried to wiggle her toes and was relieved to find they responded without any unbearable pain.

'Hard to tell. They still move but there's not much room in there anyway. Are you a doctor by any chance?'

'No, but I've seen similar things happen often before. You can only diagnose if it's a fracture or a sprain via X-ray, but if you can wiggle your toes without hitting the roof that's a good sign. Grab hold of me, and let's go. It's freezing out here.'

Once they reached the back door, she unhooked her arm from his shoulder and held on to the framework. She bent and fumbled with the zip of her boot.

He put the bunch of greenery aside.

'Here, let me help. Luckily you have a long side zip so it won't be so difficult to extract your foot.'

Kate sensed there was already some slight swelling and knew she had to get out of her boot pronto. She bit her lip and nodded.

He gripped the heel and angled the direction before he pulled it off as gently as he could. She clenched her fists but it wasn't as bad as she'd imagined. She gave him a tight smile.

'Sorry if it hurt,' he apologised, 'but if you left it much longer, you might have had to cut through the leather.' He ran his hand gently over her foot in its thick sock. 'You seem to have been lucky.'

Kate saw the funny side of the situation. She started to chuckle.

'If you think I'm lucky, then heaven help us.' She smiled at him.

Alex noticed her warm eyes flecked with gold and nodded.

'I expect so. Let's go indoors.'

'Look, I'll manage. I've bothered you enough. If I need help, I'll shout.'

He picked up the holly and extended his arm.

'I was only replenishing the logs for the day; the rest can wait.'

She gave in and took his arm; it was strong and muscled. She bounced alongside him into the living-room and sat down on a winged armchair in front of the fireplace.

He put the greenery on the table and stuck his hands into the pockets of his jeans.

'Perhaps you should get it X-rayed.'

She caught her breath.

'Oh, no! That's not necessary. Anyway, there's no hope of getting to a hospital or contacting a doctor. Apart from anything else we don't have transport, and even if we did the taxi driver yesterday said he thought he wouldn't be able to get back up to the main road without help. It doesn't hurt that much.'

He nodded.

'OK, if you are quite sure? We really

are isolated here. I tried to phone my girlfriend this morning and found we're in a black spot. I intend to go up to the main road and try again later.'

She removed her jacket, threw it on a neighbouring chair and pushed up the baggy sleeves of her pullover.

'Really? I hoped to phone my parents later, too. Perhaps connection problems are temporary because of the weather.'

He nodded, and fumbled around under the sink, extracting a red bowl.

'I'll get some snow. That will help to reduce any swelling. We'll see if that does the trick or not. If the pain continues we'll have to think about another solution.' He went off into the garden.

On his return, he placed the snow-filled bowl on the floor in front of her and she slowly lowered her foot into it. It was a temperature shock for a second before she adjusted.

'You're good at this,' she said. 'You should have been a nurse.'

He laughed.

'I don't think so. I'm too impatient.'

'I'm really grateful for all your help, but I don't want to spoil your Christmas.' Kate was beginning to like him.

He nodded.

'Leave your foot in the bowl for a while then give it a rest so that your circulation adjusts. I'll replenish the snow later. When it feels better, we can bandage it firmly to support your ankle. Don't put any weight on it now.' He tipped his forehead. 'If you're OK, I'll pop in later.'

'I'm fine, honestly. I'll sit here listening to the church service and thinking about ruined Christmas plans.'

'Ah, well! That's undoubtedly your punishment for collecting illegal holly.' He handed her the book that was lying on the table, and went out via the front door.

She did listen to the church service and she even joined in the carols because she couldn't do much else.

Glancing out of the window at the

snow-covered world outside, Kate recalled there was a golfing umbrella in the hall stand. That would come in useful as a walking stick. Once she'd bandaged her foot, she'd make the best out of the rest of the day.

She settled into the chair and picked up her book. She felt slightly foolish when she thought about what had happened.

An hour later, Alex reappeared.

'How are things?'

He'd shaved and was wearing a light flannel shirt with a brown waistcoat. As she studied his tall, slim figure, she acknowledged he was a very attractive man.

She lifted her foot from the bowl of water.

'I honestly think it is better.'

He nodded.

'Good. I'll fill the bowl with fresh snow.'

She got to her feet gingerly and held on to the back of the settee.

'I don't want to cause you any more

trouble than I have already.'

'Once you've reached the bandage stage, I'll leave you to it.' He paused. 'I don't think you've broken it. It would feel more painful if you had. If you don't object, I'll spend the rest of the morning working here. It will save me running back and forth.'

Her eyes widened.

'Work? But it's Christmas Day!'

He shrugged.

'I have a deadline to meet, and I reckoned a couple of days away from it all would be the solution.'

'Then I came and spoiled your plans.'

He smiled.

'It's not a catastrophe. We're only talking about lost minutes.' Kate found it easy to smile back at him. 'I'll fetch my laptop and carry on here. The only difference will be you on the couch.'

Kate laughed.

He grew silent for a moment and his expression was serious.

'We both expected to have a solitary

Christmas Day but fate has decided otherwise.'

She nodded and he went next door, then reappeared minutes later and arranged papers, books and his laptop in front of him on the table.

Kate didn't ask what he was doing. She settled down to finish the novel, and she left him to his work. She glanced across a couple of times and saw his concentrated expression.

When she finally shook her foot free of the bowl of cold water, the swelling had diminished visibly. He looked up.

'Better?'

'Yes. It looks and feels a lot better. There are some bandages in the first-aid kit in the kitchen. When it's bandaged you are dismissed.'

He came across to study her foot.

'Yes, I agree. It looks much better.'

Once it was firmly bandaged, he gathered his things together and tilted his head to the side.

'So, can I leave you, in the hope you won't get into any more trouble?'

She nodded.

'Apart from cooking, I'll spend the day on the couch, I promise! There's a high stool in the kitchen so I can prepare food sitting down. I bet a doctor would consider that I am being a perfect patient!'

His mouth turned up at the corners.

She suddenly had an idea how she could repay him.

'Would you like to join me for dinner? It would be no trouble. Whether I cook for one or two, it doesn't make much difference. Or have you planned something special of your own for this evening?'

He grinned.

'I was planning a cheeseburger a la mode.'

'That's settled then. About five? You'll still have plenty of time to catch up on whatever you needed to do today, and I'll feel better because I can repay a little of your kindness.'

He looked at her for a moment then nodded.

'It sounds good.'

Christmas Cheer

Kate roasted turkey breasts and added most of the vegetables she had available. She'd bought a miniature Christmas pudding and some ready-made brandy sauce at the supermarket. She decorated the table with the holly and found candles for the table and the mantelpiece. She dimmed the lighting and the room looked quite Christmassy.

She knocked on the wall just before five, and he came around a few minutes later with a bottle of wine. He glanced around and smiled.

She smiled back. He cleaned his plate quickly and they toasted each other.

'Merry Christmas!' Leaning on his arms on the edge of the table, he fingered his glass.

'Thank you! The meal was quite delicious. I hardly ever cook.'

'Don't you? I enjoy cooking when I

have the time. James used to love home-cooking.'

'James? Your boyfriend?'

It had slipped out. She hadn't intended to mention him. She nodded.

'And why aren't you celebrating Christmas with him?'

'He's history.'

'A quarrel?'

'More than a quarrel, a real bust-up.'

'What happened?'

Kate told him how she'd found him with someone else.

'Rough! How long had you known him?'

'A few months.' She took a sip of wine.

'And you're sure that it wasn't perfectly innocent?'

'I'm quite sure. He forgot I had a key. When I confronted them, she admitted right away that they'd been seeing each other for some time behind my back.'

'And it's not worth trying to patch things up?'

Kate shook her head.

'No. It's a crack in a plate. You can glue it again but it only breaks again at the slightest pressure.'

He studied her warm eyes.

'He must be a very stupid man.'

She coloured.

'And what about you? Where's your girlfriend?'

'I'm a travel writer, and I have to finish a book about Costa Rica and hand it in before the New Year. That's why I'm here. I'm starting a job as a freelance journalist for a national paper in January, so I have to get everything else out of the way. Claire would go crazy in a place like this. She's an interior designer and went off with some friends to Italy for Christmas. I decided to hide away from everyone else. I've also written a couple of thrillers, and my publisher is pushing for the next one.'

'Wow! It all sounds very glamorous to me. Don't you mind being apart from her?'

He shrugged.

'We both understand that we sometimes have different priorities. She could have come, but she decided on Italy.' He shrugged. 'We see things differently now and then, but no-one should put their partner in chains. What do you do for a living?'

'I work in an antiques shop. A very boring occupation in comparison to travelling the world or writing books. You must have seen a lot of fantastic places.' She played with her glass. 'I'd love to travel. Did your girlfriend go with you sometimes?'

He laughed softly and looked out of the window.

'She tried once or twice, but Claire thinks foreign travel should be a sandy beach and happy hour. A travel writer has to explore the nooks and crannies.' He shrugged. 'We don't even share a flat. It's not an issue, although it would be a sensible move. London is very expensive.'

Kate nodded understandingly.

'I never contemplated moving in with James. I liked it the way things were. I needed to be sure, and I'm glad that I waited. How long have you known each other?'

He played with the stem of his glass and the ruby liquid swirled and settled.

'Two years, on and off. Although if I add up the time we've actually been together it's only months. I suppose the casual arrangement suits us both.'

She shook her head.

'The exaggerated enjoyment of re-unions and sadness in partings keep the fires burning, but there must be more to it than that, otherwise you would have parted long ago.'

His teeth flashed white in the candle-light. He reached forward and topped up their glasses.

'That's partly why I gave up my wanderings, to find out where we stand, and if I want to change my lifestyle completely.' He paused. 'I've seldom talked to anyone about my plans but I feel very happy in your company.'

She grinned.

'We're strangers, and sometimes you

say things to a stranger that you wouldn't to someone you know. My best friend, Chris, tells me I prattle on without thinking and he's right. On the other hand it's interesting to peep into other people's lives.'

'True, but people are seldom completely honest with you. They want to avoid uncomfortable conversation if they know they have a different viewpoint.'

'That's where my tongue gets me into trouble, because I'm sometimes too honest.' She laughed.

He tilted his head to the side.

'That's not a bad characteristic.'

She lifted her glass.

'Here's to us and the unknown.'

He reciprocated.

'Perhaps I'll find that I love writing more than travelling and Claire and I will end up happy ever after.'

'Only time will tell.' Kate glanced towards the lane and changed the subject. 'I wanted to say hello to my family. I bet they're wondering why they haven't heard from me.'

He drank the last dregs.

'I need to phone Claire, too.' He looked at his watch. 'It's still early. I'll go up to the top of the hill to try again. Would you like me to phone your parents if the connection works?'

'Would you? That would be super. Pretend that you're James.'

He laughed.

'You were just talking about honesty.'

'I don't want to spoil my parents' Christmas. They've never met James and they never will now. I'm just postponing things. I'm going to tell them when I get home.'

'I'll tell them you'll be in touch as soon as possible and that you're having a wonderful Christmas. You can tell them we had a terrific row because his parents were toffee-nosed and he didn't support you enough.' His eyes twinkled.

'I don't think they'll ask very much.'

'Give me their number.' He got up and gestured towards the used dishes. 'Would you like me to help you clear up?'

'No, I can manage it better on my own. You'll probably get in the way.'

He stacked the dishes from the table, carried them into the kitchen and left them on the draining board. Back again, he reached for his coat.

'If you need anything, knock on the wall.'

'Thanks. It clearly wasn't a bad sprain, and your medical knowledge made the world of difference.'

He nodded, studied her for a moment in the flickering light of the candles, then turned and left.

Kate watched as he went down the path and straight ahead up the lane leading to the main road. He turned the bend and was lost to sight.

She sat on the stool and washed up. It was a little awkward but she managed. When she returned to the living-room, he was on his way back. His steps slowed when he reached her gate and gave her the thumbs-up sign.

Kate smiled and waved. He headed next door with long, purposeful strides.

She locked the door, put out the lights, grabbed her book, and hobbled upstairs. She looked out of the window.

The sun was hardly visible, almost below the horizon, and the evening sky was full of approaching darkness and the shadows were long and deep.

She thought about Alex Corbett and decided he was an unusual and interesting man; someone she enjoyed being with, and not just because he had helped her today.

She also realised she hadn't given more than a passing thought to James all day, and began to wonder why she'd been attracted to him in the first place.

Happy New Year!

Next morning, Kate enjoyed a leisurely breakfast and noticed there were dark patches along the hedges, so the snow was melting. If her foot had been OK, she would have gone for a walk, but she scrapped that idea. Her foot felt a lot better, but it was silly to take chances. She wanted to be completely mobile by the end of the week.

A little later, Alex knocked and she unlocked the door.

He came in without further invitation.

'Everything OK?'

'Much better, thanks.'

'Good! I wanted to make sure before I settle down to work.'

'Well, off you go. Get it sorted out while the going's good.' She smiled.

He smiled back.

'I still have a lot to do, but I'm hoping that a couple of days without interruption will produce a manuscript that needs editing, but no rewriting.'

Kate hesitated. She had planned to invite him to share a meal again, but if he didn't want interruption she'd keep silent. She gestured towards the snow-covered countryside outside.

'It's a pity, isn't it? You have to work and I can't go for a walk. We are both wasting a rare white Christmas.'

He shrugged.

'There will be others, for you and for me.' He stuck his hands in his pockets. 'Well, if you're OK, I'll get on.'

She nodded.

'I'm fine.'

He lifted his hand and reached for the old-fashioned door handle. He glanced back over his shoulder.

'Don't do anything silly!'

'I won't! Oh . . . was my mother very surprised?'

He chuckled.

'No, she sounded startled but she was diplomatic and didn't ask any questions. Not even how you'd sprained your ankle. She was just satisfied you were all right.'

'Mum never makes a fuss. She's saving the questions for me.' She looked at a plate of squashed mince-pies on the table and offered them. 'Would you like them for your coffee break?'

He eyed them closely.

'I feel a bit of a pirate, snaffling all your goodies, but I'm afraid it is too good to miss. I didn't think about including this kind of thing.'

She brushed his words aside.

'Professional travelling must be very different?' she asked, not willing to let him go yet.

'You need common sense and you must accept the people and the countries for what they are. It's no good romanticising all the time. You have to present the truth as you see it.

'I started backpacking round Europe in youth hostels, that sort of thing. Then after university I worked as a tour guide. When you're young, without responsibilities, it's a great life, and a good way to see the world. It was a bit of extra luck when someone asked me to write about the places I visited. Since then I haven't stopped.'

'Sounds great! I haven't been further than Europe.' She sighed. 'Most of us only ever see the world through the television.'

He looked at his watch.

'Well, thanks for the pies. I'll have to get cracking for the next couple of days. I'm leaving on Thursday. Will you be all right here on your own?'

'Of course. I'm off on Friday myself.'

'Back home in time for New Year celebrations?'

'I'm not sure if I'll be celebrating. James would have arranged for us to go to a party. Now I can do what I like. I might go to my friend Gail's party. She usually has an open house. And you'll be partying with Claire?'

'Perhaps.' There was a short pause. 'I won't disturb you any more unless we happen to see each other. I've arranged for the taxi to pick me up at nine on

Thursday, so that I'll be in time to catch the London train.' He held out his hand, and Kate took it. 'If I don't see you again, bye Kate. It's been a pleasure — and I don't say that to many people.' His eyes were contemplative. 'I don't even know where you live.'

'A small town near Cirencester. I don't suppose you've ever heard of it — Bushwarden. I've enjoyed meeting you, too. Apart from the episode of my ankle, of course, but we might never have spoken if that hadn't happened.'

He laughed softly and nodded.

'Take care!'

'You, too.'

He turned, then recalled something else.

'Do you want me to tell the taxi people to pick you up?'

'Yes, please — on Friday, about ten. I hope that I'll be able to phone them myself, but the connection here isn't reliable, and it might not work when I want it. Good luck with your book and your new job.'

'Bye, Kate, and don't change.'

'I won't!'

He closed the door softly. Kate felt a little gloomy at the thought that she would be alone for the last couple of days. He needed to finish his book, and it was clear he had to concentrate to do so.

★   ★   ★

The remaining time was good. She wasn't scared about being alone in the cottage, but she was used to hearing Alex next door. The silence made her aware of how she'd enjoyed their brief encounter. She used the time doing what she'd come to do — relaxing.

She didn't see him leave, although she heard the taxi. She stopped herself going to the window. That seemed a juvenile thing to do. They would never meet again.

A couple of hours later the owner came to clean the cottage next door and prepare it for some people who were booked for the New Year. He knocked on the door with a dark blue pullover on his arm.

'Hello! Your neighbour forgot this. Do you know each other? If you do, perhaps you can pass it on to him?'

'No, I'm sorry. We were strangers. He lives in London, but I don't know where.'

'Well, I have his address. I'll find out if he wants it sent on.'

Kate nodded and he continued.

'Is everything all right?'

'Yes, fine, thanks. I was just about to go for a walk. There isn't very much snow any more.'

'No, just bits here and there. If you follow the lane you'll come to an old watermill. The local historical society restored it. Further on, there's a side road leading to the village. Not much activity, but we have a pub and a small grocery-cum-post-office.'

'Right. I'll see how I feel.' Her ankle felt much better, but she wouldn't take any chances.

'I'll be along on Friday,' he added, bundling the pullover under his arm. 'If you've left before I arrive, leave the key where you found it under the mat.'

'I will. And thanks.'

⋆ ⋆ ⋆

Back home again, Kate hardly noticed her ankle injury any more. There was only a slight twinge now and then if she twisted on it too fast. She dumped her things, unpacked quickly, and phoned Gail.

'Kate, you're back! I thought about you several times over Christmas. Did you enjoy your solitary abode in the country?'

'Yes. I didn't miss James at all.'

'I'm not surprised. I never understood why you liked him.'

Kate thought about Alex and Claire.

'Sometimes opposite characters attract.'

'Yes, and look how it ended up for you. What are you doing tomorrow? I'm throwing my usual party. Please come.

The only stipulation is you bring something to eat and drink.'

Kate laughed.

'Who's coming?'

'No idea. I've mentioned it to everyone. I expect you'll know most of them. You know me — I never give official invites. Either people come or not. The only problem is I never know if I have enough food and drink to keep everyone happy. Someone suggested I could get round that quandary if I tell everyone to bring something.

'Last year it was great. The place was packed and my landlady kept grizzling about the noise for months after, even though I'd warned her. Come Kate, I hate to think of you huddling in your flat on your lonesome.'

'I won't huddle, no matter what I do. Is Chris coming?'

'I don't know. I told him about it, but he didn't say whether he would or not.'

They chatted about the Christmas presents they'd given and received and then the two girls rang off.

Kate decided it was time to phone her parents. Her mother answered and Kate managed quite easily to guide the conversation and tell her that she and James had quarrelled and were now going separate ways.

There was a moment's silence before her mother spoke.

'We never met him, so I can't comment, can I? You don't sound sad, love, so I presume you're not sorry?'

'No, I'm not. It was a big mistake. I'm not sorry at all. It was a waste of my time.'

'Well, as long as you feel like that, it's OK. I must say he had a very nice voice, and seemed like a very polite young man.'

Kate realised she was talking about Alex.

'Yes, he was, but he is not what he seemed to be.'

'Then it's a good thing we never met him. When I tell your dad, I expect he'll deliver his usual speech about giving him a piece of his mind. Good thing he doesn't know where to find him.'

Kate laughed.

'Would he?'

'Your father is very protective about his daughters. I'm more sensible. You'll remember that your sister had a couple of boyfriends before she settled with David. Every time she finished with one of them he made an awful fuss. It was embarrassing.

'I remember we met one of them in the middle of the market after they'd finished, and he gave the poor lad a loud dressing down. I wanted to sink through the ground.'

'Really? I didn't know that. Perhaps it's a good thing I never brought James home.'

'It is. From James's point of view, it has saved his bacon. You'll find the right one; I'm sure. Girls these days have so much more freedom. Why don't you just go out and grab someone you fancy?'

Kate laughed. He mother always managed to cheer her up.

'I'm not sure those tactics would work, Mum. I think most men would run as fast as their legs would carry them.'

'Are you going out tomorrow? If not, hop on the bus and come home. Dad and I will be watching the telly and polishing off a bottle of bubbly.'

'I haven't decided yet. Gail just invited me to her party, and I wouldn't even mind celebrating on my own for a change.'

'Well, I won't push. It's up to you. We're always here whenever you fancy a chat and a bed.'

'I know that. Thanks, Mum, and give my love to Dad, too.'

'Will do. We'd love to see you. We missed you at Christmas. Think about coming home for the day.'

'Thanks. I will.'

* * *

Kate decided to go to Gail's party. She bought a bottle of sparkling wine and left her flat in plenty of time, planning to help Gail with her preparation. This usually consisted of rearranging myriad newspapers and magazines, filling the laundry basket with Gail's discarded clothes, loading the dishwasher, and finding clean glasses for everyone.

Kate set off. The night was clear and cold. She walked along past the cathedral and noticed the light from the high windows. Someone was playing the organ and when she drew up to the entrance curiosity drew her inside.

She was surprised to find how many people were in the old church. She sat down at the back and listened to the choirboys singing, then to the words of the dean as he began the service.

Finding a hymn book left conveniently on a rest in front of her, she joined in the singing and wondered if this wasn't a nicer way to end the year than being part of a crowd at Gail's party. She decided to go home.

She was almost there when she bumped into Chris. He regarded her with amusement.

'Where are you going? I was on my way to see if you're going to Gail's party.'

'I was.' She juggled around with the bottle. 'But now I've decided I'd rather celebrate on my own.'

He looked at her in surprise.

'Really? That sounds like a great idea. Mind if I join you?'

Kate couldn't think of anyone she'd rather celebrate with than Chris. She tucked her arm through his.

'I haven't anything special to eat, but I'd love it!'

They completed the short distance to Kate's flat in silence. Once inside, Chris sauntered into her living-room while she put her bottle in the fridge.

'I intended watching 'Pride and Prejudice'. Should I forget that idea?'

He groaned but there was a mischievous look in his eyes.

'Not again! How many times have you seen it?'

'I'm not sure. A few times. I love it.'

'I know that. You must know it all by heart by now. What's the attraction?'

'Oh, you wouldn't understand. It's a fairytale, and Jane Austen's stories are all so good. If you are going to protest . . .'

He lifted his hands in surrender.

'OK, OK! Carry on. I can judge the costumes and the furnishing. Perhaps I'll learn something new.'

She made them toasted cheese and they sat companionably chatting. Kate told him about how she'd met Alex at the cottage and how he'd helped her.

Chris looked down at her foot.

'I didn't notice that you were limping.'

'I'm not. It wasn't such a bad sprain after all, and by the end of the week everything was fine again.'

He shrugged, and waved his fork in mid-air.

'I've never heard his name, have you? You're the bookworm.'

'No, but I don't read travel books very often. You usually pick up that sort of book if you are going to the place it's describing, don't you?'

They settled down to watch the DVD. For a while, Chris commented on the costumes or the furniture in the various scenes, but after a while Kate looked across and saw he was fast asleep.

The set of his chin suggested a determined streak and his mouth was firm and curled as if always on the edge of laughter.

She was almost as familiar with the clear-cut lines of his profile as she was of her own. He had acquired a polished veneer since their school days, but he was still the same dependable, confident friend. She smiled softly and let him sleep on.

The film still wasn't finished when she looked at the clock and noticed it was just before midnight. She switched it off, and shook his shoulder gently.

He opened his eyes and his smile widened.

'Did I drop off?'

'Yes, you did! It's almost midnight and I refuse to let you sleep into the New Year.' She held out her hand and pulled him up.

'I've a bottle of champagne in my bag, Leave your bottle in the fridge for another day,' he said, going to the cupboard and fetching two long-stemmed glasses.

'Yummy! What a good way to start the year.' She took her glass after Chris had poured the bubbly, and went to open the window.

She looked back on the year. Most of it had been good, apart from James. She was healthy, she had a loving family, she enjoyed her work, and she had good friends.

Chris switched on the TV and, as the last seconds of the year departed, they counted them down together.

'Happy New Year!'

'Happy New Year!' He leaned forward and kissed her.

It was light and tender as a summer breeze. A tumble of confused feelings assailed her. She was used to him kissing her cheek, but she realised suddenly that she couldn't remember him kissing her lips before. Strange and disquieting thoughts began to race through her mind, but she refused to register any significance.

She was curious to see his expression, but he had already turned and walked towards the window.

With his glass in his hand, he concentrated on the firework display and the sound of church bells ringing in the New Year. He regarded her quizzically for a moment, then the expression was his usual friendly one as he gestured for her to join him.

Unsettled, a faint warning voice whispered in her head. Perhaps her thoughts about Alex had shaken her equilibrium, or her break from James meant she'd transferred her emotional longings to the only man she'd met since then — Chris. What a silly reaction!

Mixed Feelings

The following week Kate returned to work again. Treasure Trove was in a side street off the main thoroughfare.

Her boss, Gerald, could only prosper because he'd been clever enough to buy the premises years ago, when property prices weren't so high. If he'd had to rent it, he would have been out of business years ago. Gerald lived with his wife Elaine in a rambling three-storey house in another part of the town.

Kate had a key and she wasn't surprised to find the shop empty when she arrived. She picked up the post from the floor, turned up the heat in the office cubicle, listened to the messages on the answering machine and started the coffee machine.

Half an hour later, Gerald breezed in. He was in his fifties, had a ruddy complexion and greying hair. He loved to dress in tweeds and brogues. The style suited him; it gave him a trustworthy, reliable impression and reassured wavering customers.

'Hello, Kate! Happy New Year! Did you enjoy the festivities? Any messages?'

Kate was used to his habit of stringing several questions together.

'Hi, Gerald! Happy New Year to you, too. I had a good time. No, there are no messages. I've opened the post. There's nothing urgent.'

He sighed and Kate followed his glance around the salesroom and the gaps.

'It looks like you sold some more stuff after I left,' she commented.

'Yes, mostly small bits and pieces, but it all mounts up. The small lady's desk went — someone transported it in their car. Heaven knows how they got it in. Then some man bought the stationery box. The Wedgewood meat plate went to some man who was frantic to find something unusual for a Christmas present for his wife.

'Someone else was delighted with the slightly battered coal scuttle that I wasn't sorry to get rid of, and we've seen the last of the set of those silver fruit dishes from the display cupboard. Oh! The cottage chest of drawers went, too.'

Kate took a sip of her coffee.

'I worry about burglars, you know that. You ought to do something about it.'

'We are insured, dear, and we never have a lot of silver, do we? If you like, gather up the silver every evening before you go and stick it in the safe.' He noted her expression. 'Exactly. It's not worth the bother, is it? Thieves aren't likely to advertise stolen silver on the open market, so that means they'd use the black market, or would use someone who'll melt it down. We wouldn't get it back. If we specialised in silver I'd think differently. I don't think they'd try to steal furniture — they'd make too much noise, and someone would see them.

'What's on the agenda this morning?

We aren't likely to get many customers, but you never know.'

Kate knew she had to strike when the iron was hot.

'We need to sort out some of the paperwork, Gerald. You keep avoiding it, but if we get too behind we'll get into trouble with our tax advisor and the tax office.'

He looked startled and ran his hand over his wiry hair.

'Oh, heavens! What a disgusting way to start the year. You know how I hate paperwork. Can't you sort it out on your own?'

'No, not everything. I need your signature. You are the owner of this place, although sometimes I wonder how you managed before I came.'

'I didn't. I think I gave our tax advisors heart attacks. I used to turn up with receipts, copies of bills and bank statements stuffed into plastic bags. They must have had a nightmare of a time sorting it out. Elaine was always on my back to get someone to help me in the shop. The fact that she's a lawyer didn't help. She was worried in case I was doing illegal trading and would end up in the dock one day. She nagged until the day you came into my life.'

Kate laughed.

'I can imagine why she was worried. When I took over it was mayhem. I hope I'll never see your accounts in that state ever again.'

She used her most persuasive tactics.

'Just a couple of hours this morning, please! Just imagine . . . you can then go home this evening and tell Elaine that you've started the year with a bang.'

Eyes twinkling, still grumbling and muttering, he gave in. They spent most of the morning sorting out various things and Gerald signing his name wherever necessary.

Kate had access to the shop's bank account. She'd tried in vain to persuade him to note what he withdrew or what he paid in.

He was entitled to draw out what he wanted, but Kate faced entries of sales cheques, auction house payments, his withdrawals, as well as her own salary payments.

By midday, he was looking at his watch continually and Kate knew she wouldn't be able to keep him much longer. She wasn't dissatisfied. They'd reduced the pile of work and outstanding queries nicely. The remaining ones were quite recent, so she could relax for a while.

'That's it, Kate. I've had enough for one day. I'm off to the Red Lion. Coming? They do a good steak and kidney on Tuesdays. You can tidy up the shop a bit when you get back. I'm going to put out some feelers this afternoon, phone some contacts and see if there are any house clearances or auctions in the offing.'

She smiled at him.

'No, thanks. I've brought sandwiches as usual. I can get the book-keeping up to date now. Well, almost up to date, and I have to delete stuff from our website. I'll rearrange the shop until you fill the gaps with some new acquisitions.'

Gerald got up. He sounded more

cheerful now that he could think about his lunch.

'I forgot to ask you: what did James give you for Christmas?'

'Nothing, because we broke up before Christmas.'

Gerald looked at her closely.

'You don't seem very upset. That's good. To be honest, he wasn't your type at all. He was so smooth and slick. You wouldn't be happy with a silver-tongued bloke like him. He had a brain like a calculator and eyes like a weasel. I didn't take to him.'

'Gerald! You didn't meet him very often. I'm fed up with everyone telling me he was wrong for me. If everyone thought so before, why didn't they say so earlier?'

Gerald patted her shoulder.

'Because it is not advisable to interfere with anyone who thinks they are in love.' He shrugged. 'Can't pretend I'm sorry, though. You deserve someone better, love.'

He sauntered towards the exit.

'And don't bother me with your infernal paperwork again for a while. I prefer fighting an opponent on the auction floor any day.'

The bell above the door tinkled as he lifted his hand and left. Kate smiled as she followed his jaunty step. His thoughts were already on a hot meal at his favourite pub.

Kate had Mondays off, unless something special was in the offing, and she worked until two o'clock on Saturdays. Gerald was very laid-back about her working hours. If she wanted a few hours extra, he never refused her.

She arranged to meet Gail on Saturday afternoon after work to go shopping. Gail replaced her wardrobe at the speed of lightning. She was assistant to the boss of an industrial concern and earned twice as much as Kate. She was clearly good at her job, but Kate often wondered how Gail was so efficient and organised in work. Her flat, and her personal life, were both frenzied.

Gail, Chris, Kate, and a couple of

others often joined forces and went out together. Gail didn't share the same level of friendship as Chris and Kate did, but they all got on well.

Gail viewed her friend across the bistro table.

'What happened to you on New Year's Eve?' Gail asked.

'I went to church,' Kate answered glibly.

Gail's mouth dropped open.

'It was spontaneous,' Kate explained. 'I was on my way to you when I heard organ music. I was passing the cathedral and I went inside. A service was just starting and afterwards I decided I didn't need a party after all. I had an enjoyable, domestic evening with 'Pride and Prejudice' and sparkling wine. I hope you're not mad at me. I expect your flat was bursting at the seams anyway, wasn't it?'

Kate conveniently forgot to mention she'd shared New Year's Eve with Chris. She didn't think Gail would understand why they hadn't come to her party if they were together anyway.

'It was. I don't know where all the people came from. Presumably some of them were friends of friends. The flat looked like a rubbish tip the next morning, and I was in no mood to clean it all up.'

They shared a coffee break, then Kate resigned herself to trailing after Gail and acting as her personal shopper for a couple of hours. It involved fetching different sizes, different colours, and sometimes even a different length.

The shops were busy because the sales were on and it wasn't long before they were both loaded with bulging bags.

Gail had persuaded Kate to buy a beautiful coat in a green colour that suited Kate's colouring. It was very good quality, half-price and classical in style, so Kate knew she would wear it for much longer than Gail's self-set time limit of one year.

Going past a bookshop, Gail was still chatting away, while Kate glanced in the shop window.

Her eyes settled on an announcement that Alex Corbett was holding a book signing event there in two weeks' time. She came to a halt and stared at the advertisement.

It was a nice photo of Alex. He was sitting in front of a computer amid mountains of papers and looking at the camera.

Gail turned back, seeing how Kate's gaze was fixed firmly to the window.

'What's so interesting?' she asked. 'Seen a book you fancy?'

'No, I know that man. The one in the advertisement for a thriller.'

Gail took a closer look.

'You know him?'

'I met him at Christmas. He was the man who was in the next-door cottage. He helped me when I sprained my ankle.'

Gail's eyes widened.

'You sprained your ankle? You didn't tell me that.' She considered the photo carefully. 'He's not bad looking. In fact, he looks quite yummy.'

'Don't start jumping to conclusions! He already has a girlfriend. He is a travel writer and he was there to finish a book about Costa Rica.'

'Wow! Don't some people have all the luck? I've never met anyone famous.'

'I wouldn't call him famous. He's very down to earth and interesting. If I hadn't sprained my ankle, I don't suppose we'd have spoken to each other. I was rude to him when we met.'

'Well, you must go to the book signing. Show him you're interested and send out the right signals.'

'Gail, are you listening? He has a girlfriend, and we were ships passing in the night.'

Gail pouted.

'You give up too easily.' She studied Kate for a moment. 'On the other hand, you stuck to James for a while. It's still a pity you didn't give him the push earlier. It was a waste of your time.'

Kate laughed and shoved her arm through her friend's.

'Let's go and find those boots you want.' With a last glance at the advert, she pulled Gail's arm and they went on.

When she got home, her heart beat faster as she thought about the placard in the bookshop and wondered if it would be silly to go to the signing. She scarcely knew him, but it would be interesting to see him again.

His girlfriend couldn't object, could she? They were just passing acquaintances. It wasn't strange for her to go if his tour brought him to her hometown.

Cold Encounter

Kate and Gail decided to go to the pictures and for a pizza afterwards. On the way to the cinema, they met Chris. He was fiddling with the lock of his shop.

He'd been in the fifth form when Kate started at the grammar school, but they lived near each other and they got into the habit of walking to school together. There was never anything romantic about it, even if fellow classmates teased them.

Chris left school and went to study art and design in London. He returned and started a costume hire company. He was doing extremely well and now had regular contracts with well-known TV and film companies. Recently he'd added a corner to his shop offering modern designer dresses.

Kate loved checking his stock, though she couldn't afford anything, even with the generous discount he always offered her.

He straightened when he saw them and smiled. He had twinkling eyes which seemed to view the world with humour most of the time. He was over six feet with a lanky figure and was always dressed very smartly, but not flamboyantly. Kate often thought he looked like someone who was on his way to afternoon tea in a fashionable hotel or to an exclusive cocktail party.

He glanced at Kate.

'Hi!'

Kate liked him so much it was like meeting family.

'You're late. Busy in the shop?'

He nodded and shoved a strand of hair back into place.

'Carole just left. We had a customer who couldn't make up her mind.' He turned to Gail. 'Hi! Everything OK?'

She nodded.

'Yes, thanks. I'm still recovering from my party. Why didn't you come?'

'I was sidetracked on the way.'

Gail grimaced.

'What's wrong with you lot? Kate went to church before celebrating on her own. You were diverted and went elsewhere. You missed the only New Year party worth going to in this town.'

His brows lifted.

'There's always next year.'

'Perhaps I won't invite you next year.'

He shrugged.

'Then I'll simply have to die of disappointment.'

Kate noticed he hadn't mentioned they'd been together. He'd unconsciously followed her lead. He knew Gail would start to put two and two together to make five.

'I often wondered why you didn't stay in London or go to some other big city to run your business,' Gail remarked. 'We're not exactly at the centre of the universe here, are we?'

'Too expensive. Paying for storage facilities plus shop rental would swallow the profits in a big town. The overheads are reasonable here. In fact, I'm thinking of buying the shop. It wasn't easy to get my foot in the door, but now the companies know my name, they couldn't care less where I am, as long as I supply at a decent price. Our bank manager thought I had a good idea and he gave me a decent loan to buy stock. Without that, I wouldn't have made it.'

'You make it sound easy.'

'Do I? It wasn't easy to go begging from door to door in the beginning, but that's not necessary any more. People usually contact me these days. Where are you off to?'

'The pictures,' Kate answered.

'Then we're going in the same direction. I'm on my way home. Girls night?'

Kate bent her head against the wind.

'Yes, it's a good feeling to make my own choices again. Even if I had to catch James with someone else to do so.'

His step halted and brought them to a standstill.

'You're not sorry any more?'

'No, he wasn't all I thought he was.'

Chris resumed his step and they kept pace.

'I'd heard one or two rumours about him, but it was none of my business so I didn't let the cat out of the bag.'

'Oh, Chris! You should have. I'd have been wiser a lot sooner.'

'I thought you might hate me if I told tales on your boyfriend,' Chris responded.

She laughed.

'I'd never hate you. I know you're always truthful with me.'

Gail laughed.

'I wish I knew a man I trusted that much.'

Their steps echoed. The street was almost empty.

'What about you?' Kate asked him. 'Still with . . . what was her name? Gloria?'

'Geraldine, my dear. Geraldine is also history.'

'Oh, well, perhaps there's something better round the corner for us both.'

'Perhaps.'

'Fancy coming with us? The newspapers give the film great reviews.'

'No, thanks. I'm bushed. I'm going to London first thing. Enjoy yourselves.'

They parted and the girls crossed the road.

Flicking the collar of his coat up, Chris carried on down the street in the direction of his flat at the far end of the shopping precinct. They watched him disappearing from sight.

'He is a very attractive man, isn't he?' Gail remarked. 'He reminds me of that actor, Rupert whatsisname . . . He mixes with a lot of artistic people, it's a wonder he hasn't been snapped up already.'

'Yes, I suppose you're right. I've never thought about it. Even though he works in the glamorous world of actors and films, he's still a nice person and down to earth.'

'You and Chris have always had a very special relationship, haven't you?' Gail remarked. 'You'd never believe the number of people that envy you that.'

Kate laughed.

'Yes. He's the brother I never had.'

Gail pulled off her hat and straightened her hair. Still looking in Chris's direction, she grabbed her friend's arm.

'Let's go in or we'll miss the opening.'

Later, when they were in the pizzeria, Kate mentioned she was going to Alex's book signing. Gail nodded understandingly.

'I would, too, if I knew him.'

While they ate, Gail flirted with the waiter, even though they both knew he was happily married with a horde of children.

'I love Italians,' Gail declared. 'Carlo wouldn't dream of making his wife unhappy, but he still makes every woman in his pizzeria feel she's special. I think I'll marry an Italian.'

Kate laughed. She was enjoying herself properly for the first time in ages. For as long as they were together, James had decided where they were going and when. His idea of eating out was always a trip to an exclusive restaurant where he spent ages deciding what to eat, and even longer choosing the wine he thought suited.

A couple of hours later the two girls parted to go home in different directions. Kate deliberately took a route that went past the bookshop.

She stopped to study Alex's picture again and mentally noted the date of the signing. Kate didn't imagine that Alex had masses of fans. She'd never heard his name before.

She went home with a skip in her step. The knowledge that she'd see him in a few weeks gave her a feeling of excitement.

★   ★   ★

Kate asked Gerald if she could close up early on the day of Alex's book signing.

'OK.' Gerald nodded. 'No-one is likely to call anyway. It's the wrong time of the year.'

Kate rushed home, freshened up her make-up, put on her new coat and best boots and brushed her hair until it shone.

The day was cold, but there was no wind. The high street was busy with weekend shoppers. When she went inside the bookshop, it was also full. She wandered around the ground floor and couldn't see a special group, so she went upstairs.

Looking between the various shelving, she spotted people crowding around a table in one of the corners. Alex was sitting with piles of his books and he had a microphone in his hand. Kate listened as he explained how he started writing mysteries. Then he started signing books and gradually people started moving away, clutching books to their chests.

Finally her view was unhindered. He signed and handed a book to a buyer with a smile and thanks. Holding out his hand for the next one, he looked up and their eyes met. His smile was warm and honest. He nodded at her before he began signing again.

A few minutes later, the crowd cleared and he was free. He said something to the shop assistant helping him, got up and walked towards her.

Kate's pulse increased. She felt slightly euphoric knowing that he liked her company.

He kissed her cheek briefly.

'My, you do look smart. I remember you in baggy jeans and shapeless pullovers at Christmas, but today you look great.'

'Thank you. Stop flattering!' Kate was secretly glad that he'd noticed she had made an effort.

'I'm not flattering you. I never tell lies. That always gets me into trouble.' He paused. 'I'm glad you came. I hoped you'd see the placard and call. When I noticed there was a bookshop here, I asked them to add it to the list. I couldn't get in touch, because I forgot your surname.

'It's my break. Let's go and have a coffee. They've a bistro downstairs.' He draped his arm around her shoulders and ushered her towards the stairs.

With a cup of coffee, they viewed

each other across the bistro table.

'How's the ankle?' he asked.

'Fine. It was almost completely healed when I left,' she answered, still flustered.

'Good.' He nodded. 'You're back at work again? An antiques shop, if I remember rightly?'

'Yes, it's very quiet at the moment. People are still recovering from spending too much at Christmas. It'll pick up again in a couple of weeks' time.'

He laughed and his mouth turned up at the corners.

'I tried to persuade the publishers that this was not the best time to do a book tour, but I expect they haven't anyone else who is willing at the moment.'

'And? Have you sold many today?'

'Not too bad actually.'

'I think there's always a special attraction to buy a signed book from the author, even if you haven't read their books before.' She took a sip of coffee and their eyes met. 'I remember you told me about thrillers and travel books, but I didn't register that you were famous enough to be sent on a book tour.'

He chuckled.

'I'm not. This is my second novel, but the publisher seems satisfied, and if people buy sufficient numbers it will encourage them to ask for number three. Claire won a commission to revamp a manor house near here and wanted to check the place out. When she mentioned the name of it, I hoped I might see you again. They were an unusual couple of days, weren't they?'

She nodded. Her fingers clutched the cup and she tried hard to be polite.

'Is Claire with you?' She looked around.

'She said she'd be back by two. Perhaps you'll meet her. What about your boyfriend? Have you made it up?'

'No, and I have no intention of doing so. I'm enjoying my freedom again.'

'Is your antiques shop near here?'

'Not far from here. Five minutes

away, in a side street. It's called Treasure Trove and it's not mine. I asked my boss, Gerald, for permission to close early so that I could come to see you. I normally work until two o'clock on Saturday.'

He checked his watch.

'I have to be back upstairs in five minutes, so I'll have to go.'

She gulped the remains of her coffee. Time had never gone so fast.

'Of course, I understand. I'd like a signed copy, though. I'll come with you to get one.'

He looked at her silently.

'You don't have to buy a copy, Kate.'

'I know that. Don't be silly! I do read thrillers now and then. I read a lot. All sorts of books. I promise I'm buying it because I'd like to.'

He grinned.

'The prospect of you reading it makes me nervous. When I know that strangers are doing so, it's no problem, but whenever someone I know reads my book, I'm afraid they'll think it's a complete waste of time. I'm reluctant even to send a copy to my parents.'

'Well, if a publisher thinks it's worth publishing, it must be quite decent. They don't waste their money. Let's go back upstairs so that I can get one before they're all sold out.'

He laughed and they climbed the central staircase and made their way back to the table in the corner, where the assistant was glancing anxiously at his watch.

Under his breath, Alex muttered.

'Oh, heavens! He's already counting the minutes.'

Kate picked up a book from the pile on the table and plonked it down in front of Alex.

'For Kate, please!'

His eyes twinkled.

'With pleasure.' He scribbled away. 'I've also included my home address. I'd like to hear what you think of it.'

Kate picked it up and nodded.

'Where do I pay?' she asked the assistant.

People began to gather again.

'Bye, Alex. It was great to see you again. Good luck!'

He looked over her shoulder as Kate turned to leave.

'Oh, Claire! That's good! I hoped you two would meet.'

A tall, slim, very attractive blonde woman, beautifully dressed and with impeccable make-up, came towards Alex, kissed his cheek, then rested her hand possessively on his shoulder.

Alex gestured towards Kate.

'Claire, this is Kate. I told you about her — my neighbour during my Christmas break.'

Claire eyed her and smiled at Kate, but the smile didn't reach her eyes.

'Oh, yes. Alex mentioned it. I see you've bought one of his books?'

'Yes. It was a great surprise to see his placard in the shop window. I didn't want to miss coming to his book signing. He helped me when I sprained my ankle.'

Claire nodded and regarded Kate

coldly. Alex broke the silence.

'Why don't we have a meal together later on? I expect Kate knows of a quiet pub or restaurant round here.'

Startled, Kate looked at him with questioning eyes. She didn't need to reply because Claire intervened.

'Darling, you know that's not possible. I have to leave for Paris with Michael Hamilton at the crack of dawn tomorrow. He saw some brocade in a side street shop that he thinks would suit to perfection. He wants my opinion, but I'll be home again tomorrow evening. We must leave as soon as you've finished signing if we are to get home at a decent hour.' She focused on Kate. 'Perhaps another time? I'm sure it would be fun.'

Kate looked down and shoved the book into her bag.

'Yes, I expect so.' She looked up again and noticed Alex was frowning. She didn't want to cause any conflict. 'I already have something scheduled for this evening, so it wasn't feasible anyway, but it was a nice idea. As you said, Claire, another time. I'll leave you to your fans, Alex. Bye, Claire.'

She dissolved into the crowd, thinking Claire might have invented her reason for leaving soon. Alex was clearly surprised and annoyed. On the other hand, Kate couldn't imagine spending a comfortable evening with Claire anyway. She was resentful, but why? She surely didn't believe that Alex had cheated on her at Christmas.

Perhaps Claire simply resented other women and was possessive.

From the short time she had known him, Kate didn't think that would work. Alex was his own man.

Unexpected Invitation

Kate spent most of the rest of the weekend reading Alex's book. It was enjoyable and she liked his style of writing. She decided not to contact him. If he mentioned it to Claire, perhaps the fat would be in the fire.

Monday, when the shop was closed, was her day for household chores and any other pressing business.

On Tuesday, Gerald didn't turn up until lunchtime. When he arrived, he wandered into the cubbyhole called their office. Kate was on the phone and held up a hand to block any conversation. He gathered she was talking to a customer and heard her speaking a few words in German.

Gerald parked himself on the corner of the desk.

'What was that all about?' he asked when Kate put the telephone down. 'I didn't know you could speak German. Have we sold something?'

Looking pleased, Kate nodded.

'We've sold that Victorian chest of drawers. Our internet website is paying off. The buyer comes from a place called Krefeld and I've just completed the payment. I've promised to get a quote from Danny to deliver it. I suggested they pay us for delivery, and we'll organise it with Daniel. I think they may be lucky. When I last spoke to him, he had a table to deliver to Aachen and something for an observatory on the Danish/German border. I checked where Krefeld is on the map, and I reckon he can perhaps fit the delivery into that tour.'

Gerald nodded.

'Good! Have you already marked it as sold? Otherwise someone else may fancy it. It was a decent price and in very good condition.'

'Not yet, but that's the next thing I'll do. I took German to GCSE level; I'm not terribly good, but with the help of a dictionary, somehow I manage. Luckily, the majority of Germans speak English quite well.'

Gerald brushed his hand over his hair.

'Oh, well, you seem to manage, and it's true — we have sold quite a few things via the internet since you started here. I wouldn't have set that up. Computers scare me. I wasn't in the shop often enough to cope with things like internet enquiries. Is there a cup of tea going? I'm parched.'

Kate stood up.

'I was just about to make one. Did you find anything at that house sale?' She put the kettle on and arranged their mugs.

'Yes, it was worth the trip. I have a feeling the other dealers haven't got over Christmas yet. There wasn't very much competition. I won the bid for a lovely inlaid stationery box, a small side table — which I think is late Georgian — and a set of six dining chairs. They are in excellent condition, early Georgian.

'When Sam comes in, ask him to go over the table. There's a small area of damage to the veneer on one corner. He knows how important it is to keep things original, but when Sam gives it a good clean and polish, it will look twice as good.'

Their helper, Sam, was already in his eighties and he only came in whenever Gerald thought his experience could improve a piece of furniture.

Gerald continued.

'I also bagged a couple of small oil paintings. They look quite decent country scenes to me, although I'm no expert on Victorian art. Gordon, my art expert friend, will tell us if they're worth anything. Take a couple of photos of them when I bring them in, and e-mail them to him. He can usually tell at a glance if something is worthwhile or not, and he owes me a favour.'

'Sounds like you've had a good day.' Kate handed him a mug and he took a sip. 'I'll be glad to fill the gaps in the showroom. Where are the receipts?

Hand them over before you lose them.'

Gerald put his mug down and rummaged around in his pockets until he found a couple of crumpled pieces of paper.

'Here you are. You really are a slave-driving, pernicious woman.'

'I am not. I'm just doing my job. By the way, if you find a decent cheap Persian rug somewhere, we could do with one for upstairs. I was thinking this morning that if we had a rug on the rough planking up there it would improve the surroundings no end and make it look homely.'

His eyes widened in horror, and she hurried to calm him before he could protest.

'It doesn't have to be expensive. A second-hand one will do, as long as it's big enough to cover most of the planking.'

Gerald sighed.

'Women are never satisfied. Have you ever heard of overheads? Buying a carpet for the shop is an overhead. We are in business to make money, not spend it.'

'And a businessman needs to invest to improve his chances. Appearances sell stuff. When I take photos for the internet, I even borrow Sam's dog for the picture sometimes. Most people like animals. It makes us more human.'

'Rubbish! People want a good deal. They couldn't care less about a shaggy dog.'

Kate swiped at him with the tea cloth and he ducked.

'When I've finished my tea, I'll get those chairs out of the van. Where can we put them?' he asked.

'Hmm. Six is a lot, and we don't have a dining table at the moment. Let's put one each side of the Pembroke table over there, and line the others against the wall upstairs. If someone is interested in these, I can tell them we have more of them upstairs. Find us a decent dining table. Then we can rearrange them around that later — that's if they haven't been sold by then.' Kate got up and went back to the computer on the desk. 'I'll mark the chest of drawers as sold, and then get on to Danny. I promised those people to sort things out and phone back as soon as possible.'

Gerald nodded. Heaving himself unwillingly to his feet, he went back out into the street to unload the dining chairs, two at a time.

With her own tasks completed, Kate helped him to carry some into the showroom and they both enthused over the mahogany writing box, before Kate gave it pride of place on top of a shelf in the bow window.

'Don't forget to give me your selling price, Gerald. I know how much you paid from the receipts, but I don't intend to set the selling price. That's your job. You'll only complain later if I get it wrong.'

'As long as we make a profit, it doesn't matter. Twenty percent on the chairs, fifteen percent on the side table when Sam has finished it, and between fifteen and twenty percent for the stationery box.'

Kate nodded. She loved handling old items and she loved her job.

'Right. Where are you off to now?'

'Home. I promised Elaine I'd cook tonight. I have to go shopping first.'

'What's on the menu?'

'A beef casserole and chocolate mousse for dessert.'

'Sounds wonderful. I'm amazed that you can manage such things.'

He flicked at his shoulder-length greyish hair.

'I am not just a genius in the antiques trade, my love. I am also a genius in the kitchen. Why don't you join us? Elaine keeps on about inviting you around for a meal. She seems to think I should be grateful to you. She believes no-one else would put up with me as a boss for longer than a day. She tells me to pamper you.'

Kate laughed.

'That is a very good idea. She's right — no-one else would put up with you.

Thanks for the invite. Another time. I'm going to the pictures with a friend this evening.'

'Well, I can tell Elaine that I tried. I'm off. Bye.'

* * *

The shop was quieter than normal for the first couple of weeks of the New Year. They did have some customers, and someone bought the stationery box, but most of the people who came in were tourists looking for something to do to kill time, especially if the weather was bad. Kate got the paperwork up to date, rearranged the stock, and generally tidied the place up.

One afternoon she was entering sales when the phone went.

'Hello. Treasure Trove, Kate speaking.'

'Hello, Kate. I'm glad I've got the right telephone number. Alex here.'

She caught her breath, recognising his voice.

'Alex, what a nice surprise.' She paused for a moment. 'How did you find our number?'

'It's easy these days. Just ask a computer. I don't know your address, but I remembered the name of the shop. It reminded me of 'Treasure Island'.'

'I see.' She gripped the phone tighter. 'What can I do for you? Are you looking for an antique?'

He laughed.

'No. Although I like antiques, I just can't afford any. I have an ulterior motive for getting in touch.'

'And that is?'

'My publishers are holding a special dinner for the authors of books they published last year, and I'm invited.'

'Nice for you, but what has it got to do with me?'

'It's an unspoken stipulation that we come with a partner. Claire is on a commission to renovate a manor house, and she's too busy. I've already asked her and she said it was impossible. If it were taking place in the Bahamas she'd probably make an effort, but a dinner by a lesser-known publisher in a London hotel doesn't attract in the same way.'

'Oh. Can't you just turn up on your own?'

'When I talked to the organising secretary she hinted that if I don't come with a partner they'll supply someone from the company, someone I don't know who'll probably resent having to go with me.'

'Can't you skip the dinner altogether? Is it so important? Have you got to go?'

'They're hoping the evening will create extra publicity. They've invited contacts, critics, and anyone they think important in their corner of the publishing world. They also want all of their current authors there, smiling into the camera.'

'And?'

'And — I thought of you right away. We could spend an enjoyable evening together.'

Kate swallowed hard and was glad he couldn't see her expression.

'Are you serious? I know nothing

about publishing.'

'I don't know much, either. I only went on the book-signing tour because Claire persuaded me it would do wonders for my image. I didn't enjoy it much and I don't think I'll agree to another one for a long time. I won't be able to anyway — if I have to produce a weekly column and start producing my next book as well.'

His invitation whirled inside her confused brain.

'What's your column about?' she asked, playing for time.

'The editor wants information linked to current news. He tells me what the main articles are about, and expects me to fill in with description of fringe happenings and local colouring. That means the main story could be about anything: about a starlet who is living it up in Los Angeles, about burgeoning conflicts, unemployment in the Hebrides, or religious strife. He wants my article about the area involved if I know it. He puts it somewhere on the same page.'

'It sounds like an interesting idea.'

'I think it might be very interesting, because no two weeks will be the same. The editor gives me the subject a few days in advance, but sometimes he needs something overnight.' He recalled why they were talking. 'Well, what about it? Will you come?'

She swallowed hard.

'I don't think it is a good idea, Alex. We don't know each other very well, do we? Don't you know someone else? What about sisters, cousins, or former school friends?'

He burst out laughing.

'I don't have any sisters. I'm not mad about my cousins, and I've lost contact with former school friends. I've been moving around too much to cultivate old friendships.'

Kate remembered Claire's expression when they had met in the bookshop.

'It's so unexpected. I'd like to think about it. Are there dress rules of some kind? When is it?'

'I know I'm springing it on you.

Think about it. I'll phone you tomorrow evening if you give me your home number. As far as I know it is a formal do, but you wouldn't need a long dress or that sort of thing — just a nice dress. It's in three weeks' time, on the fifteenth. I'll pay for your hotel, of course. I'd like to see you again, and you immediately jumped to mind when I knew I had to find someone.'

She had a slight reprieve; time to think about the pros and cons. She still didn't understand why he'd thought of her, but she'd think about the offer. She gave him her number.

'Good! How are things?'

'Fine, thanks — and you?'

'Me, too. I should have been polite and asked you that straight off, but I wanted to settle my problem and strike when the iron was hot. I'll call you tomorrow evening — about six. I really would like you to come. It will make my evening bearable. Please come!'

Despite knowing it was an extraordinary request, somehow Kate felt elated.

Even though they barely knew each other, he'd thought of her, and hoped that she'd say yes.

Something Borrowed . . .

That evening, when they were having a cappuccino after the cinema, Kate told Gail about Alex's request. Gail brushed the froth from her lips then held the cup between her two hands.

'Good heavens!' she exclaimed. 'I didn't realise there was anything going on between you two.'

'There isn't!'

'Are you sure that you didn't share more than a Christmas meal when you were snowed in at Christmas?'

'Of course not! Alex helped me the day I sprained my ankle, but I left him alone after that because I knew he was working.'

'I still think it's very surprising. Didn't you say he had a girlfriend?'

Kate nodded.

'Yes. She's an interior designer and tied up with work on that day — well, that's what he told me.'

'Hmm, a bit strange, isn't it? Normally any girlfriend would make an effort, wouldn't she?'

'That's what I reasoned, too. So what do you think? I like him, but if he already has a girlfriend . . . '

'Yes, I see what you mean. It's like casting your fishing line into a pond where you know there are no fish.' She put down her cup with a clatter. 'On the other hand, why worry about his girlfriend? If she can't be bothered, he has a plausible reason to ask you and it'll be an interesting evening. Go! It's a one-off invitation and if he pays for your hotel, you've nothing to lose.'

'He's nice, and I don't think there is anything sneaky about him asking me. If he wanted to try something on, he wouldn't go to such lengths, would he?'

'You can always get up and run if he oversteps the mark. He knows you'll mention the invitation to other people, and he's not stupid enough to spoil a serious relationship with his girlfriend just for a fling. I think his girlfriend is stupid not to make more of an effort, but perhaps she's convinced it'll be utterly boring.'

Kate's forehead creased.

'The business with his girlfriend bothers me, but I have to believe him.'

Gail studied her carefully.

'Quite honestly, I think you want to go, don't you? You just want me to encourage you.'

Awkwardly, Kate cleared her throat.

'Yes, perhaps that's true.'

'It's a pity that he's not available, because you seem to fancy him. Still, it will be a special night out and I'm glad you're moving on after the James catastrophe. By the way, I'm going to arrange a foursome next week for us to go bowling.'

Kate's expression fell.

'Don't argue or say you don't want to come. I'll organise someone nice. I've got my eye on someone in the office, and as soon as I've persuaded him, I'll get him to bring someone along for you.'

Kate laughed.

'Gail, you are incorrigible!' Somehow, Kate felt relieved. 'Help me chose what to wear?'

★   ★   ★

When Kate asked Gerald for the day off, he was nosey enough to ask why and what for.

She explained.

He viewed her speculatively.

'You're going up to London to see someone you hardly know? Spending an evening with him at some fancy do, and he's paying for your hotel?'

Kate nodded.

'Of course you can have the day off, but it sounds fishy to me. You don't go around inviting young girls on outings like this. What's his name again? I'll look him up, and if I find there is a hint of scandal, I'll refuse permission.'

'Gerald, you are not my father. It is nothing to do with you. Either give me the day off or not.'

'Oh, all right, but don't do anything foolish. I was relieved to see you dump that other chap, even though I hardly knew him. I don't want you ending up with another undesirable bloke.'

'He isn't undesirable; he has a serious girlfriend. I'm just a stand-in.'

'That's not very flattering, is it? Doesn't it bother you that you are second choice?'

She picked up some papers and started to walk towards the door.

'No, because I like him. There is no misunderstanding between us. Before you warn me, I am not likely to disappear without trace. Too many people know where I'm going. I'll be back at work the following Tuesday, as usual.'

*　*　*

When Alex rang to find out if she would come or not, he sounded delighted when she said she would.

Later that week, Kate spent an

exhausting evening with Gail, because Gail insisted that they practise her make-up for the evening. Kate hadn't intended to emphasise her features so much, but in the end she admitted that extra eye make-up and added skin colouring improved her looks no end. She normally used make-up sparingly, but an evening in London with Alex called for more glamour.

Alex had mentioned it would be good if she wore a cocktail dress. Gail insisted she should use her connections and ask Chris to help. Kate tried to resist, but Gail dragged Kate into Chris's shop one day when they were out and explained that they needed an appropriate dress for Kate and why.

He hesitated, and under his steady scrutiny Kate felt slightly uncomfortable. She wondered if it was fair to ask Chris for his professional help.

She noticed how his square jaw tensed and his eyes lost all traces of amusement.

'Are you sure this man is OK?' he

asked. 'He's an author I've never heard of.'

'He writes travel books, mysteries, and he's just starting to write a column for a newspaper.'

Without further comment, Chris turned on his heel and crossed the room. He searched through the rail and held out a designer dress in shades of bronze, with a crossed bodice and pencil skirt.

'Try this. You can borrow it for the evening.'

Gail looked at Kate and then at the dress. She nodded gleefully.

'Perfect.'

Chris had worked with clothes too long not to know exactly what suited. When she tried it on, Kate loved the way it emphasised her figure and highlighted her creamy skin. It looked fabulous on her. She hardly recognised herself in the mirror, but she was still reluctant to borrow it. She glanced at the price ticket.

'What if it gets damaged? I can't

afford to replace it.'

Chris studied her, and no matter what negative thoughts he might have had, he seemed pleased with his choice. He tried to reassure her.

'We'll worry about that if it happens. By the way, we are experts in stain removal. It looks good on you. Enjoy it.'

'But I must give you something for borrowing it. How much?'

Chris ran his hand through his thick hair.

'Oh, don't worry about that. I wouldn't do it for anyone else, you know that. Don't look a gift horse in the mouth.'

Gail piped in.

'I don't understand why you don't just accept Chris's offer without all this quibbling. You've been pals for yonks. It's not as though you are going to run off with it or deliberately damage it.'

Chris nodded.

'True. I know what I'm doing.'

'I've seen the price tag. I've never worn anything so expensive.'

Getting impatient, Gail turned to Chris.

'Don't pay any more attention to her. Put it in a bag or a box, Chris. It's the only way. She needs a pair of matching shoes, and they'll take ages to find.'

With a final backward glance, and without further comment, he packed it into a box and handed it to Gail.

A few minutes later they were on their way down the high street. Even though she went on protesting, Kate was secretly looking forward to wearing something so beautiful. The dress fitted her to perfection.

They found a pair of reasonably priced high heels that Kate could wear later on in the summer.

'You are wasted in that antiques shop,' Gail said back at Kate's flat when she tried the whole outfit on again. 'No-one sees you. It's like sticking a rose in the middle of a potato patch. Are you sure you wouldn't like me to find you another job?'

Kate twitched the skirt into position,

still amazed by the difference clothes could make.

'No, I would not,' she retorted. 'I'm happy with Gerald in the shop. Don't keep on!'

'You could earn three times as much elsewhere.'

'I'm not interested! I'm happy where I am. I'm practically my own boss, and I earn enough for my needs.'

* * *

Kate travelled up to London by bus. It was cheaper and she wanted to relax. She hadn't visited London often, although she always enjoyed herself when she did.

She decided to take a taxi from the bus station, as she had a small suitcase. When she arrived at the hotel, she found Alex had reserved her room as promised. She freshened up and decided to use some of the remaining time to visit a place of interest.

She chose the Victoria and Albert Museum, because she'd never been there. There was too much to see, and after a couple of hours she decided reluctantly to go back to the hotel. There was no point in rushing. She needed time to get ready.

As seven o'clock approached, she checked her make-up again, gathered her coat, and picked up her clutch bag. She came downstairs in the lift.

When the doors glided open, her eyes wandered around the foyer and halted when she saw Alex standing near the reception desk. He spotted her, his smile broadened and he strode across to her.

'Wow! You look great. Is this the same girl who enjoyed spending time in baggy pants in an isolated cottage in the country?'

She coloured slightly.

'You look pretty good yourself.' Her glance took in his perfectly fitting tuxedo, tanned skin, and skilfully cut hair.

He held out his arm.

'Shall we? It's just around the corner.

Claire always complains if I suggest walking anywhere, because she's afraid of spoiling her hairstyle.'

She tucked her arm in his.

'In her job, initial impressions are important and she probably needs to impress a future client from the word go.'

'Maybe you're right.' He looked down at her and gave her a warm smile. 'And once again, thanks for coming.'

Perfect Gentleman

It was a delightful evening. The publishers had organised it perfectly. There was subdued lighting, beautiful table decorations, good food, and delicious wine.

Kate sat between Alex and another author who explained he wrote about long-forgotten civilizations and their culture. He was in his late fifties and needed no encouragement to tell her about his journeys of discovery.

Kate was genuinely interested, and with Alex on her other side the evening couldn't go wrong. A photographer circled the room taking pictures and Kate smiled at the camera when requested.

After the opening speeches finished, and the meal was underway, her neighbour drew her into conversation again. Now and then Kate and Alex also had time to chat. The editor-in-chief wandered between the tables in the middle of the various courses. He stopped to talk to Alex, who introduced her as his friend Kate.

Now and then Alex discreetly pointed out some well-known authors among the other guests.

'Gosh, it's like being at the opening night of a movie!'

He exchanged a smile with her.

'Not so glamorous, I'm afraid. Even if people know a name, few readers bother to find out what an author looks like.' He grinned. 'I don't think anyone will ever pester me for an autograph.'

She returned his grin.

'You never know. If you're writing for a national newspaper and producing mysteries, someone might invite you to a breakfast show or something. Then you won't be able to buy bread and milk without someone recognising you.'

His expression warmed as he studied her face.

'And I'd be famous at last! I don't

think so.' He gestured around. 'I realise that publishers need as much publicity as they can get; they have to sell their wares. A lot of authors may love getting involved in publicity, but I don't.'

'But you aren't the average author, are you? You see things differently because of your travels. That's influenced your attitude. You are multi-faceted and unconventional. That'll make you an interesting interviewee.'

His brows lifted and the corner of his mouth lifted.

'You're quite a philosopher. I'm not sure if I like being analysed in that way.'

Her expression was flustered.

'I'm not analysing you. I am only pointing out why you're not the usual run-of-the-mill author.'

His dark eyes twinkled.

'I understand what you mean, and you are right. I don't even know if I can stick with journalism and writing mysteries yet. Up to now I always thought life was too short to be stuck in a box.'

She sighed.

'Most people have no choice. Responsibility, loyalty and contentment get in the way.'

'We should reach out and grab our opportunities.'

'But that involves being egotistical and ignoring any plans or wishes of people you know. We're not all happy to drop everything and head off into a glorious sunset.'

His brows drew together.

'Perhaps not, but people don't always want the same things from life. Is it irresponsible to choose freedom instead of duties or obligations?'

'No, not irresponsible, but it is self-centred.'

He laughed softly and his face relaxed.

'If you came with me on one of my journeys, I'm sure you'd see my point of view more clearly.'

She coloured at the idea and chuckled.

'I've never wanted an unpredictable,

abandoned lifestyle. My friend Gail would love it. I'm too faint-hearted. I'm happy in my low-paid job in an antiques shop in the English country-side.'

He looked at her questioningly.

'And how do you see your future?'

She shrugged.

'If I'm lucky, I'll find Mr Right, get married, and have a couple of children and live in the same place with the same people all my life.' She met his glance. 'You undoubtedly find that a very dreary prospect.'

He laughed then studied her care-fully.

'No, not dreary. Traditional. But people like you keep the wheels turning; I just need a new direction more often than the average person.'

Kate wasn't sure if she should be offended.

'OK, I'm old-fashioned, and I don't mind if you think so.'

Her words intrigued him.

'You're conservative, but that doesn't

132

mean you are old-fashioned. I don't know many who are as honest as you are. People of our generation think they're missing out if they don't change their job or their partner every year or two. You seldom hear anyone admit they're looking for a partner for life.'

She shrugged.

'And a lot of people chase rainbows all the time and end up with second best because they keep thinking there is something better round the corner. I thought my ex-boyfriend was for me, but I now realise there is no point in pretending. If you are lucky, you find someone for life, and end up like my mum and dad.'

Reluctantly he nodded.

Kate's neighbour on her other side caught her attention and she had to turn away.

'My dear, I've just been thinking. Do you suppose that your boss could find me an antique writing desk? A small one, suitable for my mother. It would be a wonderful surprise for her seventieth birthday.'

Kate nodded.

'I'm sure he can, if he knows your financial limit. Give him a ring one afternoon. I'll give you his mobile number.' She scribbled it on a serviette and he thanked her and pocketed it.

The rest of the evening remained entertaining. Various publishers and authors gave speeches and told humorous tales of their trials and tribulations in the course of their profession.

When Alex walked her back to her hotel it was noticeably cooler and she glanced up. The stars were twinkling far above them and the moon was bright.

On the way to the hotel entrance, they chatted about the evening, and she was a little nervous because she hardly knew him and hoped the evening would end on a good note and not an embarrassing one.

'Would you like a nightcap?'

She shook her head.

'No, thanks.'

She was almost relieved when he

leaned forward and kissed her forehead gently.

'Then I can only say thanks for being the perfect partner, Kate.'

Flustered, she smiled.

'Thank you for inviting me. It was a stimulating insight into the world of books and writing.'

He thrust his hands deep into his pockets and his dark eyes were unfathomable.

'We'll keep in touch?'

She hesitated, remembering Claire.

'Yes. If you're ever in the area give me a ring and we can meet for a coffee or something.'

'What about tomorrow morning? We could meet up for a walk or something before you leave?'

Kate didn't feel happy about the idea of meeting him again so soon.

'I'm leaving quite early, so I can't, but it was a lovely idea.'

He nodded.

'OK. Have a good night's sleep and a good journey home.'

'I will. Bye, Alex! Best wishes to Claire, and perhaps we'll meet again one day.'

The mention of Claire's name did the trick. He shifted and nodded silently.

Kate turned away and walked towards the lift. She turned to wave as she waited for it to arrive. He was still standing there. When the lift doors opened, he lifted his hand, before he headed for the exit.

In her room, while removing her make-up, she thought about the evening. There had been no awkward moments and he'd behaved faultlessly.

She folded the dress carefully and put it aside. It would go on top of everything else between tissue paper.

She decided she'd visit the National Gallery before she caught the bus home tomorrow. It would give her the chance to study some pictures more carefully, and perhaps understand what Gerald sometimes talked about when he discussed portrait painting.

Close Companions

On Monday morning, Kate took the dress back to Chris's shop. His assistant Carole took the box and unpacked it. She clearly knew that Chris had loaned it, but didn't comment. She checked it carefully. Kate had checked it herself and it had been on a hanger ever since she got home.

Carole nodded.

'That looks just fine. We'll get it dry-cleaned — but we do that with any items that we've loaned for productions.'

Kate nodded.

'I was so grateful.' She looked around. 'Is Chris out? I wanted to thank him again.'

'He just popped out, but he won't be long.'

'I'll hang on for a couple of minutes, just in case.' She looked at the dresses hanging in the recesses of the long room and noticed for the first time how it was organised according to colours and sizes. 'So many clothes.'

Carole smiled.

'Oh, this is just a small selection of what Chris has on offer. The rooms out back are packed, and Chris has a small warehouse full of costumes on the edge of Morton's Field.'

'Golly! Where did he get it all?'

'I think he started out by buying up old period dress from auctions or house sales, and we still have quite a lot of them, but they have drawbacks. Women had much smaller waists in those days, and it wasn't always possible to alter them properly if there was a lot of beading involved. Replacing beading is a very expensive business. That's when Chris started making his own things. Not literally, but he has a couple of women who sew to the designs he gives them.'

'He designs them himself?' Kate commented, surprised.

Carole nodded.

'He uses illustrations from fashion magazines going back as long as they've been around, and he gets ideas for earlier costumes from portraits of that particular era.'

'It must be a painstaking job to produce historical clothes. Some of them are very elaborate.'

The door opened and Chris came in. His expression lifted when he saw Kate. He deposited a bulging canvas satchel on the floor.

'Hello! How did it go?'

'It was very interesting. I sat next to someone who explores ancient tribes and their settlements. He's been to some unusual places. Alex was on the other side, so between them I was completely entertained. The food was good, the wine flowed, and the whole evening went well.'

He looked at the clothes racks briefly and asked no more.

'Good.'

'Alex complimented me on the dress.

It gave me a lot of confidence. Thanks, Chris.'

He brushed her thanks aside. He hesitated for a moment.

'It's your day off, isn't it? The weather is super at the moment. How about a break? Anything special need my attention here, Carole?'

Carole shook her head.

Chris came across and tucked his arm through Kate's. He picked up his satchel again and guided them towards the door.

Kate went willingly and they chatted about London. He knew it a lot better than she did and he talked about places she'd never seen as they walked down a side street to a quiet cul-de-sac.

There was a bricked circular flower-bed in the centre of the group of old buildings. At present the central patch was full of daffodils and narcissi. They waved in bands of yellow and white in the mild breezes.

They sat down on the brick edging of the flower-bed and Kate lifted her face towards the sunlight.

'Oh, for the first time this year I really think spring is on its way.' She looked across at Chris and was aware just how much she enjoyed being with him. Their friendship was so uncomplicated.

Most people said they had difficulty knowing where they stood with Chris. People couldn't make up their minds if he was just being polite, or if he was keeping them at arm's length to shut them out. Since he'd established his business that characteristic had intensified.

Kate knew a completely different character. When he smiled, his expression was like sun breaking through depressing grey clouds. Sometimes, especially recently, she had felt their friendship was on the edge of something else — something that she couldn't define and which she chose to ignore.

Today gusts of wind blew his unruly hair around and he kept pushing it back into shape with his long fingers. Kate had always loved the understated way he wore his clothes.

He was a friend in every sense of the word. He always gave advice or gentle encouragement whenever she needed it most.

After university and his stay in London, he'd come back and established his business in the high street. They'd never lost touch, even in the times when he'd been elsewhere.

'You look pleased with yourself.'

'I just heard that I've won the contract to supply a Victorian TV play. I'm intending to sort out what I can suggest they use later on this afternoon.'

'Good for you! Was there a lot of competition?'

'There aren't that many hire companies with our capacity, but I did wonder if I would get it. I was not very polite to the director when he started showing me photos of costumes he thought might be suitable. They were often from the wrong period.'

Kate laughed and he continued.

'I realise that I'm sometimes anti-social, crabby, and tetchy. I have to remind myself every so often that I must be pleasant to prospective customers — especially when they are insincere, hollow, or phoney. Unfortunately, in the artistic world of films, TV and the theatre, there are a great number of phoneys and I have to watch my step. I almost gave in to him just to get the contract, but I decided agreeing to non-authentic costumes wouldn't do my future business any good. In the end, I told him he had good suggestions but they didn't fit. I showed him what I had in mind. I thought I'd lost it, but this morning he phoned and said we had the contract.'

'It goes to show you were right to stick to your guns. Perhaps it was a test.'

'Yes, ma'am, you're spot on! He told me so when he phoned.' The laughter lines on Chris's face deepened. 'I try to be honest, and at the same time I've learned how to be obliging, understanding, and persuasive. I don't think many people notice that I am sometimes manipulative.

She nodded.

'If you were a bootlicker, I wouldn't like you any more. I know you have to yield a bit now and then because of your business, but I know you'd never overdo it. You wouldn't be my Chris if you did.'

He chuckled.

'You actually like me! I couldn't risk losing that, could I?'

There was an air of efficiency and self-confidence about him that had always fascinated her. She leaned back and was still for a couple of moments with the sun on her face and her eyes closed. That was why she liked being with Chris — they never had to play-act with each other and talk non-stop. She heard muffled sounds and she opened her eyes.

Without more ado, and with the sun

dancing on their faces, he passed her an earpiece from his Smartphone, and they sat side by side listening to a group who were unknown to Kate. She suddenly realised she could only do something like this with Chris. Other men would not have sat quietly by her side as they listened and waited for the music to end.

When it finished, Chris was smiling at her. He leaned down and reached for a small paper box in his satchel. The box contained two pastries, oozing with cream and topped with raspberries and shreds of coconut.

Her mouth dropped open.

'Oh, those look scrumptious, but I can't. I've put on weight non-stop since Christmas and my waistband is getting too tight. I have sworn to stop eating sweets, biscuits, and pastries for a while.'

He waved the box under her nose.

'Stop making excuses. Go on, have one.'

She tried to push the box away.

'No, don't tempt me.'

An expression of mischief covered his face for a moment. He took one out and pressed it against her lips. The cream oozed, and she struggled to catch the raspberries with her tongue before they tumbled down her chin and on to the front of her jacket.

Avoiding any more imminent mess, she grabbed the rest of the pastry from him and devoured it quickly. She wiped across her mouth with the back of her hand and then, before he had time to register her intention, she took the other pastry and shoved it against his mouth in the same way.

She caught her breath as she watched his face. There was something hidden at the back of his eyes for a couple of seconds that she couldn't interpret.

The blue was flecked with grey and the amused look suddenly disappeared. It wasn't often that Kate didn't know what he was thinking.

He clasped her wrist and took the pastry out of her hand. He broke her thoughts, chuckled, and her sense of humour took over. She laughed. He stared at her for a moment and joined in. He finished the pastry in two bites and rubbed his hands together.

'Kate, you have cream on your nose.'

She wiped the offending spot and grinned in good humour.

'I have to go. I have to do my washing and housework. I always do it on Monday.'

'Like my mother. How boring!'

'Ah, but then I have a clear conscience for the rest of the week. You shouldn't comment. You have a cleaning lady and you take your shirts to the cleaners.'

He threw up his arms.

'Guilty, your honour! But housework and cleaning is boring, isn't it?'

Standing, she straightened her shoulders.

'Of course it is, but it has to be done, or we'd end up living in a dump. Thank you for my impromptu lunch break. I loved the music, I loved the cream cake, and I loved the time we shared together.'

He made a sweeping gesture with an invisible hat.

'It was my pleasure, and I enjoyed it just as much. It took me back to our days walking back home after school. Remember how we used to call in at the baker's on the way and buy a cream bun if one of us had enough money?'

She smiled.

'Yes, and I also remember that you always ate most of it. At least you didn't shove it in my face in those days!'

'In those days, I would have thought it a waste of glorious cream. Do you remember how we tried once to make them ourselves in your mother's kitchen? We made a terrible mess. Your mother reminds me of it almost every time I see her!'

Kate spluttered.

'It seemed an easy recipe at the time. I think we ruined one of my mother's saucepans in the process.'

'Is there a chance that she'll forgive

and forget if I buy her a new saucepan?'
He stood up and pushed his hands
deep into his pockets.

She laughed.

'After all this time? She constantly
reminds me of the day I passed my
driving test and you came around with
your battered Ford. She was worried to
death when you persuaded her to let
me drive to the coast.

'It was my first long journey, my
nerves were shattered by the time we
got there and it wasn't even worth the
trip. The sky was slate grey, the pebble
beach was murder on the feet, and even
when we reached the solid sand beyond
the pebbles, we still had to walk a long
way to the water's edge, only to find the
sea was freezing cold.'

'Ah, but the fish and chips were
delicious, and the trip gave you enough
confidence to cope with driving from
day one, didn't it?'

She laughed, got up to join him, and
straightened her jacket.

'Trust you to remember the fish and

chips. I'll see you!'

He lifted his hand.

'Yes, see you!'

Kate turned away and walked around the circular flower-bed to take a short-cut through an overhead arch linking two blocks of houses. She walked home, enjoying the feel that spring was on the way, and life was good. Her mouth curved into an unconscious smile.

Chris watched her until she was out of sight. He brushed at the remains of the flaky pastry and headed back to the shop.

As he went, his thoughts were busy with the past and he had to remind himself there were important tasks waiting. He had to sort out some suggestions for the TV production.

Angry Accusations

Gail phoned to ask about Kate's London trip. She didn't ask too many questions, so Kate presumed her friend thought there was romance involved.

Gail announced she'd organised a foursome on Sunday to go to the pictures and a meal afterwards. Kate wasn't enthusiastic about the idea, but Gail was only trying to be kind, so she gave in. Gail then also tried to persuade her to join her fitness club and come with her to learn Scottish dancing the following week. Kate turned both suggestions down.

Then Gail suddenly remembered she had something else to tell Kate.

'Do you know that there's a photo of you in 'Publishers' Weekly'?'

'Really?' Kate said. 'No, I didn't. I didn't realise you read publishing magazines.'

'I don't, but someone in the office showed me an article about a book we both read recently and I saw your photo, amongst others, on the opposite page. Gillian is a bookworm and we have similar tastes. She recommends books to me now and then. I can't be bothered to haunt bookshops to find what's worth reading.'

'I must get a copy as a souvenir. Is it the current issue?'

'I don't know. I'll ask Gillian if you can have hers when she's finished with it, if you like. Save you the money.'

'Yes, please.'

'OK. See you on Sunday. We'll meet up in front of the cinema at six. That'll give us time to see the early show and plenty of time to go for a meal after. I suggest we go to the Red Lion for that. The only decent restaurants around here are too expensive and on the edge of town.

'Oh, by the way,' Gail continued. 'The two chaps are Roger and Lance. I've paired you off with Lance. He's more your type; quieter and more conservative.'

* * *

Later that week, Kate was filling in time in the showroom. She dusted various pieces of furniture and rearranged things in the display cabinet. When the old-fashioned bell over the door tinkled, she looked up, expecting to see a customer.

To her utter surprise, it was Claire. She looked like a model who'd stepped off the front page of 'Vogue'. Her cream-coloured outfit was deceivingly simple in style, her spindly bronze high heels were eye-catching, and she carried a handbag that shone like a freshly harvested chestnut.

Hiding her surprise, Kate managed a smile.

'Claire! What brings you here? Are you looking for an antique for one of your customers?' She couldn't think of another reason.

Even though the room was already

full of enough shadows, Kate could tell there was an additional warning cloud forming across Claire's features. Kate wondered apprehensively what was coming. Claire had made it plain in the bookshop that she saw no reason to be friendly. She hadn't made a journey to the shop today unless she had a good reason.

Kate didn't have to wait long to find out why.

'No, I'm not looking for an antique,' Claire snapped. 'It's nothing to do with business. If we needed antiques, I wouldn't come to a shop like this one. Do I have to spell out why I'm here? I think you can guess.'

To her annoyance, Kate found herself starting to colour.

'No, I'm sorry. I can't,' she said, confused.

Claire moved closer until they were face to face.

'Come off it! Don't pretend to act the innocent with me. I'm here to tell you to stay away from Alex.'

They stared at each other for a moment until Kate recovered. She swallowed hard and then found her voice again.

'I don't know what's bothering you, Claire,' she said tersely. 'I saw Alex at the book signing and was with him that evening in London. Just those two times.'

'Are you stupid?' Claire demanded, her voice rising. 'I'm talking about how you spent the weekend with Alex, and got your picture in the paper with him at that dinner. A working colleague found it in a magazine and showed it to me this morning. He knew that Alex and I are a twosome and he couldn't wait to rub my nose in it. Leave Alex alone and stop chasing him!'

The colour drained from Kate's face.

'Don't be silly, Claire. Alex explained you couldn't attend and asked me to substitute. It was a perfectly harmless evening. I am not chasing him.'

'Don't call me silly! You stayed in a hotel room that he paid for. I have access to his account and I checked.'

Kate's skin grew hot then cold, and her stomach tightened.

'Alex only asked me because you were busy elsewhere. It was a perfectly innocent invitation.' Kate heard the sarcasm in her voice.

'Do you deny that Alex paid for the room?' Claire's lips puckered with annoyance and she went on with a sardonic expression.

Growing anger was gradually overriding Kate's confusion and uncertainty.

'I'm not denying Alex paid for the room,' Kate retorted heatedly. 'It was his way of saying thanks for my help. We spent a pleasant evening together and that was it. We parted in the hotel lobby and I didn't see him again.'

'Huh!' Claire's accusing glare spoiled her beautiful features. 'I had a funny feeling that day at the book signing, and afterwards when I asked him about how you two spent Christmas at that cottage. I think you've had your eyes on him since then. Well, let me warn you,

Alex is no different from any other man, but I also know how he ticks. You don't.'

Disconcerted, Kate crossed her arms and the colour rose in her cheeks.

'I am not chasing Alex. Ours was a chance meeting at the cottage. I don't deny that we get on well, but there is nothing romantic about our relationship. If you don't trust him, why didn't you agree to go with him? You put your job first, then you're surprised when he looked for an alternative. He told me the publishers expected authors to bring a partner. He asked for my help. I helped.

'I didn't see Alex again after he left me at the hotel after the dinner. I came home on Sunday afternoon. Is there anything else you want to know? Otherwise, please go now. You are being childish, and very offensive. Sort it out with Alex and leave me out of it.'

Claire hesitated, but with a glare that was still brutally unfriendly. Her brows heightened and, without answering, she marched to the door and flung it open. It shook in its frame when she slammed it behind her.

Kate stood immobilised by shock for a moment. Some trick of the subconscious recalled her memories of the moment she'd discovered James was two-timing her. She felt just as humiliated and embarrassed now as she did then.

She noticed that her hands were shaking and her mind still reeled with confusion and surprise.

A fragment of sense gradually emerged and she began to sympathise with Claire a little. Perhaps Alex hadn't explained properly how important the evening was for him and Claire only realised it now and was lashing out at her. It was also understandable why Claire might believe his invitation wasn't purely platonic.

Kate needed some fresh air to clear her head. She grabbed a bundle of cheques to pay into the bank, hung the 'Back soon' sign on the door and left.

Taking a shortcut to the high street, along a little lane that ran behind the church, she gradually calmed and noted that spring was evident everywhere and the sun was shining through the burgeoning green on the trees.

The air was fresh and cool and she breathed deeply as she went along. Her thoughts circled around Claire's visit and her unfounded accusations.

The bank was busy and she had to wait, but it felt good to be amongst other people, and not sitting in the loneliness of the shop wondering if it was her fault in some way.

Once she left the bank, she looked at her watch and wondered if she should take a lengthy lunch break in one of the busy bistros and prolong her return a little longer.

Deep in thought, she jumped when she heard her name.

'Kate!'

It was Chris, and she had never been happier to see him. He was always her rock in a storm.

He joined her and she gave him a tentative smile.

'What are you doing gallivanting along the high street at this time of day?' she aked.

He smiled.

'I could ask you the same question.'

She forestalled an answer with a shrug, but the question was in the air, so she gave a quick reply.

'I've been to the bank.'

He nodded and viewed her speculatively.

'Is that all? You look all het up to me.'

'Do I?'

Throwing up his hands, he sighed.

'I've known you too long. What's wrong?' He reached out and touched her arm. 'Look, let's have a cup of coffee. Is there an emergency at Treasure Trove?'

She shook her head.

'No.' The prospect of talking to Chris about Claire's outburst was appealing.

With his hand under her elbow, they headed for the nearest bistro. Once seated and their coffees ordered, he unwound his long scarf from around his neck and put it aside.

Kate knew that other women found him attractive. Even back in their school days she was aware how school friends envied their friendship. His features were not classically handsome, but something about him was compelling, and even nowadays she noticed the extra glances he gathered from other women.

He'd had a couple of serious girlfriends, but none of them had lasted very long. He never talked about any of them, and Kate never asked. It was an unspoken rule that they didn't interfere in each other's love lives.

'What's bothering you?' he asked.

Her intention of not talking about Claire's visit wavered and collapsed. She told him the whole shebang, right up to Claire's appearance this morning.

He knew who Alex was, where they'd met, and that she had gone up to London to see him, so it wasn't all completely new information.

Their coffees arrived and Alex cradled his cup as she ploughed on. When she paused, his eyes were sharp and assessing as they searched her face.

'And? Is there any truth in her allegation?'

'No, of course not. It was all completely innocent. Just a pleasant evening together.'

'Are you sure that's all there was to it?'

The colour flooded her cheeks.

'Of course I'm sure! I thought you knew me better than that.'

He shrugged.

'Sometimes sanity flies out the window when emotions are involved.'

She cut in on his words.

'I like him, but that doesn't mean I lose all sense of propriety.'

His mouth tensed.

'His minor celebrity status could easily sweep all good intentions aside on a special evening like that.' He paused for a second. 'If you have nothing to feel guilty about, I don't know why you're bothered. She got the wrong end of the stick and acted like an elephant in a china shop.'

'I know — it's just the shock of her accusing me like that. I don't know whether I should contact Alex and tell him what happened or not. What do you think?'

He shrugged.

'That's up to you. Follow your instinct. I don't know him so I can't judge. Perhaps she won't mention that she came here now that you've denied it.' There was a faint glimmer of humour in his eyes when he continued. 'On the other hand, she may like putting him on the spot. If so, it might be kind to forewarn him that she's on the warpath.'

Kate already felt better. Just talking to Chris helped to put things into perspective.

'She was so ferocious when she faced me in the shop. I expected her to go for my jugular any minute.'

He grinned.

'Sounds like she felt like a woman scorned. Will you phone him, then?'

She looked up at him again.

'I'm not sure if I have his telephone

number. If so, I'll phone him. If not, I'll leave him to his fate.'

He nodded and winked.

'OK. Feeling better now?'

'Much better. Thanks, Chris.'

'Nothing to thank me for.'

'Have you never had a confusing experience with a girlfriend like that?'

He held her glance for a moment.

'Not exactly similar, but yes, there was someone. She belonged to someone else, and I didn't realise I liked her that much until it was too late. That confused me quite a lot for a while.'

Kate was surprised. She'd never considered that Chris might have relationship problems. The idea that he could fall in love with another woman bothered her.

She realised suddenly that any girlfriend he had was entitled to dislike their friendship. She held her breath for a moment then managed somehow to sound reassuring.

'Well, you've never lacked for adoring females. I'm sure you'll find Miss Right one of these days.'

'Who knows?' He glanced at his watch. 'Ready? I have to be back in the shop by two. There's an important phone call in the offing.'

Kate finished the last dregs of her coffee and stood up.

They walked side by side, as far as Chris's shop, then Kate stood on tiptoe to kiss his cheek silently before she carried on and went down the next side street.

Chris stood for a moment and watched her disappear. Thrusting his hands deeper into his pockets, he entered the shop and told Carole she could take a long lunch break.

* * *

One afternoon the following week, Kate spotted James on the opposite side of the street.

For a brief moment, she was flustered, but then realised any kind of real feelings she'd had for him had died. She was glad. She was grateful and happy that she'd found out in time.

She noted how he paused when he saw her, and how extra colour flooded his face. Kate managed to nod before she carried on.

She could have ignored him totally, but she mused they were likely to meet from time to time and he was now just a former acquaintance.

Kate didn't see his reaction; if she had, she would have seen a fleeting expression of regret.

That evening Gail tried to persuade her to go on another foursome with the same two men as before, but Kate put her off. She had enjoyed the previous outing with Lance, but there had been no spark. Perhaps it had to do with meeting James, but Kate began to muse that relationships were more complicated than anyone expected.

She was glad that she was free of emotional involvement at present, and she had no desire to change the situation.

Say It With Flowers

On Friday morning, as Kate approached the shop, she noticed someone was standing in the doorway with his back turned towards her. Somehow, the figure was familiar.

Her pace lessened and he turned. It was Alex. He was clutching a bunch of red flowers.

Kate's stomach knotted for a moment, then she cleared her throat.

'Good heavens, Alex. What are you doing here?'

He shrugged his shoulders and stuck out his hand with the flowers.

'I want to apologise for Claire. I don't know exactly what she said, but she told me she'd been to confront you. I can imagine she wasn't very polite.' He thrust the flowers towards her. 'My apologies.'

Kate had no alternative but to accept

them. She turned the key and opened the door.

'Thank you, but it's completely unnecessary. Come in.'

He followed her through to the office.

'Hang up your coat and grab a chair,' she said. 'I'll make some tea.'

She busied herself with finding a vase for the flowers. Their vibrant colour cheered the surroundings. He sat and watched her.

'I'm so sorry, Kate. I still don't understand why Claire came here to accuse you before she talked to me. I explained at the time that the publishers wanted us to bring a partner so they could calculate the catering figures. I mentioned it to her weeks in advance. Either she didn't listen, or she didn't understand how important it was.

'At the time, there was no reaction or comment. When I noticed she'd filled her calendar with another commitment for that evening, I began to think of alternatives and immediately thought of you.'

'You don't have to explain. If anyone should apologise, it's Claire. I hope she hasn't sent you?' Kate busied her hands with pouring the tea and indicating towards the milk and sugar.

He shook his head.

'I came because I was angry when I found out she'd been here before she even talked to me.'

The bell over the door tinkled and Gerald's heavy footsteps announced his arrival. His surprise was evident when he came into the office and saw them.

'Oh! It's not often we get visitors in the office. I'm Gerald Townsend. I gather that you are a friend of Kate's?' His brows lifted and he waited.

Alex got up and held out his hand.

'Alex Corbett. Yes, I'm a friend of Kate's. I'm here to clear up a misunderstanding.'

Gerald shook his hand and nodded.

'You're the author fellow Kate mentioned, aren't you? Well, carry on, don't let me stop you chatting. I just popped in to see if there was anything needed before I leave for an auction later on this morning.'

'As far as I know there's nothing,' Kate told him. 'There was no post this morning, so you should be OK. Alex and I were almost finished anyway. I'll get you a mug of tea, too, shall I?'

Alex butted in.

'I know it is a bit of a cheek, but could I borrow Kate for an hour or two? I'd like to clear the air properly. Perhaps I can take her to breakfast somewhere?'

Gerald viewed them both for a moment.

'Go ahead. I have to leave at eleven for the auction rooms, so as long as she's back before then, it's fine with me.'

Kate lifted her brows and viewed Gerald pleadingly as she handed him his mug of tea. It didn't have the slightest effect.

'Try the Red Heart,' Gerald suggested. 'They do a decent breakfast buffet between eight and eleven.'

Alex nodded, put on his coat, retrieved Kate's and held it demonstratively in her direction. Kate gave in.

She led the way. He admired some of the buildings in the old part of the town as they went along.

Once they were sitting in the spacious dining-room of the Red Heart, he looked around.

'Nice place,' he commented.

Kate nodded.

A waitress hovered in the background and supplied visitors with coffee or tea. The food on offer was arranged temptingly on a long refectory table at the end of the room. Kate hung her bag over the back of her chair.

'Shall we?'

Alex followed her, and whereas Kate chose a small bowl of mixed fruit and some toast, Alex came back with a cooked breakfast. He made himself comfortable, and reached for the cutlery.

'It's too much of a temptation!

Usually I only have a bowl of cornflakes. I caught the early train and I haven't had anything to eat since last night.'

Kate managed a smile, buttered her toast, and nodded understandingly. At this moment, she could only think that he was an exciting and unpredictable man. He had come all the way to apologise for something he hadn't done. A telephone call would have sufficed. Not many men would go to such lengths.

'Tell me about the town. Did you grow up here?'

He tucked in to his breakfast and Kate obliged with information about the town, and about herself, between her toast and spoonfuls of fruit. He was a good listener and asked the right kind of questions. He sounded as if he was genuinely interested.

Kate began to wonder what she wanted of him and, more importantly, what he wanted of her. Did Claire know he was here this morning? It didn't look like it. He hadn't mentioned her apart from wanting to apologise for her behaviour.

He told her about his current article in the newspaper. It was about the hopeless situation of young people, a lot of them highly qualified, who were looking for a job in Tunisia. Kate made a mental note to buy the paper occasionally just to read his contribution.

They were sitting in a window alcove. She looked up and saw Chris coming along the pavement outside. His casual glance met hers and she smiled. The beginnings of a smile tipped the corners of his mouth until he registered she was sitting with someone he didn't know. His smile dissolved into a brief acknowledgement. He moved on quickly without a backward glance.

Alex noticed him, too.

'Who is that? A boyfriend?'

'Chris. He's my oldest and best friend. We've known each other since our school days.'

'What does he do? He's too well dressed to be a blue-collar worker.'

'Chris has his own business,' she replied, surprised that Alex made that kind of distinction. 'He specialises in hiring out period costumes for film and TV productions. Apparently he's doing very well.'

Alex nodded, finished his meal, and poured himself another cup of coffee from the jug standing on the table. He eyed her carefully.

'Do you ever come up to London? Shopping sprees — that kind of thing?'

Kate shook her head.

'No, not often. I don't earn enough to go on shopping sprees in London. I'm happy with our local shops.'

'Well, why don't you make an exception? If you do, I'll meet you and take you for afternoon tea in the Savoy.'

The suggestion was so unexpected she was lost for an answer for a moment.

'Claire won't be pleased if you did that.'

He shrugged.

'Claire created an unpleasant situation and I would like to recompense.

I'm not Claire's property. There is nothing wrong with meeting someone I know. I've never complained about all her business trips. I could get just as uptight and question her loyalty. I don't, because I am not the jealous type.'

Kate was silent for a moment and looked down at the tablecloth. She met his glance before she ploughed on.

'But she is, Alex. Otherwise, she wouldn't have come to see me. Does she have reasons for feeling that way? Something that happened in the past?'

He threw back his head and laughed.

'I'm no angel, but I'm not Casanova either. I thought we understood each other. I was often away on my travels for months on end, and that never bothered her. Now that I'm more permanent, she is more possessive than ever. People say that marriage has had its day, and people only want to live together, but the fact remains that people like Claire want to formalise things, and I'm not sure that's what I want. I don't like being pressurised into deciding one way or the other.'

Kate shrugged.

'We're all different. I think women want a permanent situation more than men because they are predestined to have children.'

'You'd be shocked to see how many women in this world are left to cope with children on their own because the men have left them to it. Men have a primitive hate of being chained.'

'That doesn't make it right. It's what I call having your cake and eating it!'

He laughed.

'It'll take a long time for that situation to change. Will you think about coming up to London? It would be a chance for you to visit a gallery or a museum. You might even want to go shopping after all. If you do, ring me and I promise I'll take you out to tea. It's yummy at the Savoy!'

His invitation confused Kate. She wasn't sure what to make of him. He admitted he was in a steady relationship with Claire, yet he saw no harm in engaging someone else's interest.

He had charisma, he was interesting, he had an exciting background, and his interest in her was flattering. There was nothing unique about herself. James had taught her a lesson. She should be more cautious and selective.

Kate looked at her watch.

'I have to go, Alex. I promised to be back at the shop before eleven.'

He nodded.

'It's fine. I'm just glad I had the chance to talk to you and tell you that I was sorry for the way Claire acted. I like you, Kate. I have ever since I met you. You are different.'

Her cheeks were warm and she didn't know what to say. She stood up.

'Thank you for the lovely flowers. Are you going back to London, or have you something else to do locally?'

'Nothing special. I'll take a stroll around the town. The habit of exploring places where I am will never fade. I know there's a train to London just after one, so I have an hour or two to fill in.'

She nodded and hoisted her bag to her shoulder. He stood up and leaned down to kiss her lightly on her cheek.

It was gentle and impersonal. Kate smiled.

'Thanks for the breakfast and have a safe journey.'

'Will do, and don't forget to think about visiting London soon. I'd love to see you again.'

Kate just nodded and hurried out. Her brain was too confused to notice anything as she turned the corner into the high street and joined the morning shoppers on her way back to Treasure Trove.

When she passed Chris's shop she looked in. He spotted her and came to the door. He held on to the framework with one hand.

'Who was that? A customer you had to entertain?'

They never needed to avoid the truth.

'No. That was Alex. He's the chap who was in the next-door cottage at Christmas. The one who invited me to that dinner in London.'

There was a spark of some indefinable emotion in his eyes but he didn't ask another question.

Kate knew instinctively he wanted more information.

'I told you how his girlfriend came here recently and accused me of trying to pinch him. He turned up with some flowers and an apology this morning.'

Chris gave an impatient shrug.

'And? Are you trying to pinch him?'

She sensed his disapproval.

'No. Don't be silly!'

His voice was carefully neutral.

'Seems a long way to come from London just to give you a bunch of flowers.'

She blinked hard and tossed her head.

'You're surprised that some men think I'm worth the bother?'

His features were a mask and he

didn't reply. She lifted her chin and met his reproving eyes without flinching. It wasn't often that they jarred. Kate felt this could be such a moment if she talked any more about Alex.

She wouldn't tell him Alex had suggested meeting again. He would disapprove; she knew that instinctively.

She glanced briefly at her watch.

'I have to go. Gerald is waiting. He's going to an auction somewhere.'

Chris gave her a bleak, tight-lipped smile.

'OK. See you around.'

'Yes. Bye!' She turned away and disappeared into the shopping crowd.

When she reached the Treasure Trove, Gerald was sitting in the office, his feet on the desk and his nose in the newspaper.

He got up quickly and the chair swung back into an upright position again.

'Oh, good! You're back. I wondered if you'd remember. He's very refined and stylish. Anyone special?'

Kate could tell Gerald hadn't taken to Alex, either. It was strange that Chris and Gerald were sending out negative signals about him.

'No, he's no-one special. Just a friend.'

'A friend that buys you expensive flowers — still, it's none of my business.' He grabbed his coat from the back of the door. 'I'm off.'

Kate nodded and was busy with her own thoughts as she watched Gerald leave.

In His Kiss

In the end, fate decided. One of the Victorian paintings that Gerald had bought at the house clearance sale a couple of weeks ago had wakened the interest of the pal of Gerald's who was an art expert. They'd sent him photos, but he wanted to take a real-life look and suggested Gerald should bring it up to London.

Kate impulsively gestured when she heard them discussing it over the phone. He covered the mouthpiece with his hand.

Alex's suggestion popped into her mind, and she told herself there was nothing wrong with having tea with Alex if he had time to meet her.

'I was thinking of going up to London next Monday. If you like, I can take it with me. It's not very big.'

Gerald nodded gratefully and arranged the details with his friend, Gordon. He wrote down the address and handed it to Kate.

'I'll cover the cost of the taxi and your train journey, that's the least I can do. If the painting is by the artist Gordon believes it is, he'll keep it and put it into an auction on Victorian painters. If it's worthless you'll have to bring it back!'

Kate nodded. As soon as Gerald went out, she phoned Alex.

He sounded delighted when she said she was visiting for the day on business, and they could meet afterwards if he still wanted to.

He promised to reserve them a table for three o'clock.

She put the phone down and sank on to the nearest chair. She tried to ignore a rising sense of panic as she wondered if she'd done the right thing.

★   ★   ★

On Monday, Kate reached the station forecourt in plenty of time. Brown paper covered the painting and there was enough string to make carrying no problem. She met Chris coming out. He stopped in his tracks when he saw her.

'Where are you going?' He looked at her parcel. 'Delivering an item?'

'Yes, and spending a day in London. Gerald is paying my fare, and Alex has invited me to tea at the Savoy.'

His brows straightened and he frowned.

'Alex? Again? Is that sensible? I thought he had a green-eyed girlfriend who didn't like you.'

'Yes, that's true,' she said as casually as she could, 'but Alex invited me. I don't think Claire minds. He must have mentioned it to her.'

Chris shoved his hands deep into his pockets.

'Isn't it asking for trouble unless you know what she thinks about it? It's not like you. Does he have such a hold over you? Are you keen on him?'

Kate coloured.

'Don't be silly! Alex is a friend. I didn't ask him if Claire is coming. Perhaps she'll be there, too.'

'I don't know him, but I find it odd. If he has a steady girlfriend, why pay you all this attention?'

His tone infuriated her, because that was what bothered Kate, too, but she was too obstinate to admit that to him.

'You're right. You don't know him, so don't pass judgement!'

Her remark hardened his features. He took his hands out of his pockets and lifted them in defence.

'OK! OK! Do what you like, but don't come bawling to me if you find out he's not all you think he is.'

She glowered at him.

'I won't! If you'll excuse me now, I have to go.'

He made a sweeping gesture with his hand.

'Don't let me stop you.'

He glared at her before she set off at a fast pace for the station forecourt just round the corner.

Chris couldn't see it, but when she reached the platform, she swallowed hard and bit back tears. They'd squabbled about unimportant things through the years now and then, but they had never parted in real anger.

She'd never felt that she'd alienated him as strongly as she did at this moment. He was annoyed with her and he'd given a negative opinion about someone he didn't know. They were at loggerheads, and she wasn't sure how she'd casually breach the gap later and make everything right again.

As she waited for the train, she breathed deeply. She hoped that her trip would settle the question of whether she should keep contact with Alex in the future, or avoid any more contact of any kind.

She would pay attention to her instincts.

* * *

The journey was uneventful and a taxi deposited her outside Gordon's house.

He was expecting her.

Offering tea and biscuits, he left her with his wife and took the picture to his workroom. Kate and his wife chatted and filled in the time until Gordon came back. The smile on his face told her the journey was worthwhile.

'It's genuine! Trust Gerald to spot it. This artist is fetching good prices. These scenes of cows drinking at the village pond and rustic labourers in the background aren't everyone's idea of art, but the Victorians loved them. Gerald said I should clean it up if it's genuine. I will, then it won't look so gloomy. It'll bring several thousand pounds.'

'Gerald will be pleased. And I'm glad I don't have to carry it back home.' Kate got up. 'Thank you for the tea. I'm going to look at the Turner exhibition and I'm meeting someone for tea this afternoon.'

Gordon nodded.

'I'll be in touch with Gerald about the details. Are you going shopping?

That's what our daughter does whenever she comes.'

'No. Not enough time — or money.'

He laughed and accompanied her to the door. He watched her set off down the street.

Kate took a deep breath and looked forward to the rest of the day. Her confrontation with Chris was still on her mind. She could remember without the slightest effort every detail of his face. He'd been a part of her life for too long. She hated to disagree with him.

She enjoyed the exhibition, although she didn't have time to study many of the pictures carefully.

Checking the time, she could see it was still a little early, but it was better to be early than too late. Her mind was a crazy mixture of hope and fear. How strongly was she attracted to Alex? He was another woman's man.

A wave of apprehension swept through her as she exited Charing Cross. It only took her five minutes to walk to the Savoy.

Alex was already waiting outside.

She smiled when she joined him.

'You're early, but that's good.' He leaned down and kissed her cheek. 'You look very smart.'

Kate coloured, more aware of him than ever.

'Thank you.'

He put his hand under her elbow and they went into the tearoom.

Kate looked around and was glad she was wearing a stylish outfit. A white blouse peeped out of her jacket and softened the classical lines. He was wearing a dark sports jacket and navy chinos. His blue and white striped shirt was open at the throat.

Alex glanced around, looking at a neighbouring table.

'Isn't it a pity that even when people know they're coming here they don't dress accordingly?'

Kate looked around and up at the domed glass ceiling that flooded the room with natural light. She shrugged.

'Some people don't know any different,

and some of them may be multi-millionaires in disguise. You can't change the whole world.'

He smiled and nodded.

'You're right.'

The waiter arrived with finger sandwiches, scones with jam, and some slices of sponge. He arranged them skilfully on the table and asked what they wanted to drink. He went off and returned with cocktails in elegant long-stemmed glasses.

'As ordered, sir.'

Alex lifted his glass.

'Here's to us.'

Kate toasted in his direction.

'What luxury! Here's to us, and thank you for the invitation.'

He gestured towards the food.

'Help yourself. If you'd rather something else, just say the word.'

She shook her head.

'Heaven forbid! This is perfect.'

They shared the food and Alex told her about a row he'd had with his editor the day before.

'But I've also managed to finish

chapter two of the next book,' he added.

'Do you know how it will end when you start writing?'

He shook his head.

'The story develops as I go along. I just know what crime, and how it happens when I start. Did you come up just for our tea, or have you been shopping? I don't see any bags.'

Kate told him about the picture and that it was worth several thousands of pounds.

'Gerald will be over the moon when I tell him. A find like that doesn't happen every day, and he worries constantly about overheads. This will give him breathing space for a while.' She moved a crumb from the corner of her mouth with a fingertip and smiled at him and his mouth twitched with amusement.

'You are wasted in that shop. You mentioned that you don't earn much. What's your boss's name again? He doesn't appreciate you.'

'He's called Gerald. I'm sure he

does, even if he doesn't tell me so. He hates office work, so I do all that for him and I run the shop when he goes out searching for new wares. He can't afford large wages. I know, because I'm in charge of finances.

'He's generous in other ways. He gave me a beautiful Georgian side table last year on my birthday. I have it in my hallway. It is worth a bob or two. I am also learning a lot about antiques. I was always interested in history, so I'm doing something I enjoy. You can't always measure things in pounds and pence.'

He eyed her carefully.

'If you like I could ask some people I know in the trade. I'm sure there are antiques shops in London who would pay you much more, and then you'd be at the centre of things.'

'Thanks, but no thanks. I'm happy where I am.' Kate recalled briefly that Chris hadn't enjoyed London. He said it left him disillusioned and dissatisfied. 'Perhaps I'd earn more, but I'd need to pay more for accommodation and other things. My family and friends are where I am now. London is wonderful — all the art galleries, museums, history, and unusual things that are here — but it's not for me. I need the same place and the same people in my life every day.'

He reached across and tipped up her chin with his finger, looking deep into her eyes.

'You are unusual and quite special, Kate,' he said softly.

She coloured and his finger dropped away.

'I'm not. It's all a matter of what you enjoy.'

They chatted about books and the latest films. Kate discovered that he didn't own a television, and that he missed freedom of travelling.

Time flew and when the dishes and cups were empty both of them said it was the best afternoon tea they'd ever had and Kate thanked him.

Outside they stood and looked at each other for a moment.

He glanced at his watch.

'It's still early. Would you like to see where I live, or have you booked a ticket home already?'

Kate was tempted as he smiled warmly down at her. The smell of his aftershave was attractive and wafted across to her. If she took a later train it would make no difference. There was no-one there to meet her.

'Yes, I'd like that. As long as Claire doesn't mind.'

He ran his hand over his face and grinned wryly.

'We have separate flats. Mine is often in a muddle, hers is not. I'd like you to see where I live.' He took the decision out of her hands and flagged down a passing taxi.

A couple of minutes later it stopped outside a three-storey Victorian house. Kate didn't ask where they were.

He led the way up two storeys of stairs, unlocked his door, and stood aside.

Inside he held out his hands for her

coat. His gaze lingered too long on her face. Kate was by no means blind to his attractions and suddenly knew that it wasn't such a good idea to come here after all.

He folded her coat and put it across the back of an available chair. She looked around. The room had high ceilings and all the walls, where visible, were white.

His voice drifted over her shoulder.

'I have two rooms and a bathroom and it costs the earth. Just a bedroom and this living-room. There's a built-in kitchen in the corner.'

The so-called kitchen wasn't larger than a cupboard, and the cooking facilities were minimal. He followed her gaze.

'I eat out mostly,' he explained, 'or cadge a meal from Claire. She has a spacious flat. It's aesthetic and sophisticated, with never a thing out of place. I need to unwind and not worry about crumbs and a bit of disorder. That's a bone of contention between us, and why I hang on to this place.'

Kate was glad that he'd mentioned Claire. It made her feel her visit wasn't so fraught with danger.

'That is a tough nut to crack. If she is very tidy and you're not, you'll end up having constant arguments.'

'Yes, I think so, too. Claire tries to ignore the differences, but I see trouble on the horizon. When I came home on a brief visit it didn't matter, but it's different now. I'm not sure where we stand any more. Somehow I don't think you mind a bit of a muddle.'

Kate felt a little breathless.

'Oh, I like things to be tidy, too. If your place is a dump when you come home, it's depressing. My friend wastes hours searching for things because she drops everything wherever she happens to be. Afterwards, she can't remember where, among all the chaos.'

She looked around and gestured.

'Your place isn't too bad. I've seen messier ones than this one.'

'That's because I tidied it this

morning. I'm not talking about mere tidiness. You can eat off Claire's floors, it's so sterile, and nothing is ever out of place. It's uncomfortable. I'm even afraid to disturb the cushions.'

She couldn't help wondering if he and Claire did match. Their attitudes were so contradictory.

'Where did you meet?' she asked.

'In Hong Kong. She was on holiday, and I was seeing how much it had changed since it was returned to China.' His head tilted and he studied her carefully. 'You know how it is sometimes . . . Claire was relaxed because she was enjoying a holiday, and I was glad to meet a beautiful British woman in foreign surroundings. We clicked.

'The differences became evident after she returned. When I came home on short visits, it didn't matter, but now that I'm here permanently, the problems are there all the time.'

Kate couldn't understand why they stayed together if both of them knew they were so different. Was Claire hanging on to something that didn't exist any more? Was he trying to ignore the situation for some reason of his own?

She cleared her throat, didn't comment, and concentrated on the room. A multitude of books with colourful covers filled the shelves of one wall. There was a music centre with a collection of old-fashioned records, and some exotic-looking pictures of places she didn't recognise.

A couple of striking sculptures were scattered here and there and a desk was in front of the only window. He gestured to the leather couches, facing each other, with a glass table in between.

'Make yourself comfortable.'

'I like your flat; it's got character.'

He hastily removed some socks from a corner of the couch.

'What would you like to drink? I've got coffee, tea, and red or white wine.'

'A glass of white will be fine.'

He poured two glasses and came across. Handing her one, he flopped down next to her and fondled the glass in his hand.

Kate was acutely conscious of his long, lean form. She took a hasty sip of her wine.

'You're sure that Claire doesn't mind me being here?'

He put his glass down on a side table and reached across to take her hand. Kate was so surprised she didn't have time to snatch it away.

He fondled the back of her hand with his thumb and she swallowed hard.

She realised that she liked him, but he wasn't what she wanted. His aura, his attraction, blinded her, but she was sure he wasn't the love of a lifetime.

She began to wonder how to distance herself. He was sending signals that Kate understood, but didn't like. Her breath caught in her throat.

Her silence only acted as a stimulus, and he reached for her shoulders. His mouth covered hers and the kiss was slow and thoughtful. Kate immediately knew that her ideas about him were just fanciful pipe dreams. She didn't want him to kiss her.

He spoke with desperate firmness.

'I've wanted to do that for a long time. In fact, I can imagine us together on a more permanent basis. I'd love to travel the world with you. You'd bring it all to life for me again, and make it more exciting.'

Kate swallowed hard and felt incapable of facing a situation she hadn't properly envisioned. They hardly knew each other.

Reality kicked in and told her that he was nice, but he was wrong for her. She didn't need uncertainty and adventure.

She put her glass on the table and forced her lips to part into a stiff smile.

'That's a very daredevil idea. You're joking, of course! You've only recently stopped your travelling career. You have Claire, your job, your writing.'

Her reaction seemed to amuse him.

'Why is it hard for you to believe I'd give it all up for you? Sometimes things happen in our lives that we can't control. There's something about you that tells me it would be worthwhile.'

His face neared hers again and when he tried to kiss her again, she turned aside and his lips brushed her cheek. Embarrassment began to replace her uncertainty.

'You don't know me. We've spent next to no time together.'

'When we start seeing each other regularly, all the rest will fall into line. I've never experienced anything similar before. I even tried to ignore it, but I keep thinking about you.'

She shook her head.

'I'm sorry. I like you as a friend, but nothing more.'

He stiffened slightly.

'Then I seem to have misunderstood the situation completely.'

She flushed miserably. What a rotten judge of character she was! She'd assessed James wrongly, and now Alex was expecting something of her that she didn't want to give.

'Alex, I didn't want to give you the

wrong impression. I see now that I shouldn't have come with you.' Her face was hot. She was conscious of his scrutiny for a moment, before he pulled her towards him again, and although Kate tried to dodge his kiss, he held her face firmly between his hands and kissed her anyway.

Kate pushed him away, rubbed the back of her hand over her lips and struggled to her feet.

The animation left his face. There was a look of sadness because he realised what was coming.

'I think this is one of the moments in my life that I'll look back on and wish I'd handled better. Forgive me, Kate. I didn't ask you back here with the wrong intentions. I wish we'd met at another time, in another place and without any entanglements. I might have had a chance.

'I have to sort things out between Claire and me, but somehow, even if I had, it wouldn't have made any difference, would it?'

She shook her head regretfully.

He ploughed on.

'I've known for ages that things were not right between us, but I let it drift because it was more convenient. Basically we have different aims in life.' He got up, his shoulders hunched. She felt sorry for him.

'I'm very flattered that you are attracted, but we are also very different. You know that, too, don't you? Perhaps you misunderstand your own feelings because you and Claire are mixed up right now.'

He shook his head.

'It's more than that.'

Kate shrugged.

'I just happened along at an emotional low moment in your life. I thought we were friends, and even though friendship sometimes leads to something stronger, that hasn't happened. I like you, Alex. I don't want to hurt you.'

He managed a weak smile.

'I don't want friendship. I wanted more. I wish you felt the same way about me, but you don't.'

She shook her head.

'I hope you find the right person, at the right time, and a love that lasts. Good luck with your work and with your life. I'll find my own way out.'

She turned away without waiting for a reply, grabbed her bag and coat, slipped through the door, and clattered down the stairs. He didn't follow and she was grateful for that.

Outside, daylight was fading. She took a deep breath and asked the first passer-by for directions to the nearest tube station.

Feeling confused on the journey home, she mused that she couldn't even talk things over with Chris when she returned.

He had warned her not to come running.

Shock Discovery

Gerald was delighted with her news that the painting was quite valuable and could be auctioned soon.

Gail rang with good news, too. Her voice was excited and she hurried breathlessly to tell Kate.

'I think I've met him.'

'Who?'

'My dream man. He works for the management advisory board in London. I thought he would be dry as a packet of porridge, but outside office hours he's great fun. He's intelligent and talented. He's also good enough to take home to my parents.'

'Good heavens, then he must be special. You've never thought about doing that with any of your previous boyfriends, have you?'

'No. It sounds mad, doesn't it? It didn't take five minutes until I knew he was the one.'

'My, my! You are serious, aren't you? It's great news. And he's just as smitten?'

Gail giggled.

'Yes. He's only here to sort out some hiccups in the company, but I'm hoping I can persuade him to apply for a management job here. If not, I may think seriously about moving to London.' She paused. 'I rang because we had arranged to go shopping tomorrow, but . . . '

Kate laughed.

'It's off? I don't mind.'

'He's only here until the end of next week, and we want to see each other as much as we can until then.'

'Then go ahead! I'm happy for you, Gail, and I hope that he deserves you.'

'We can meet one evening next week, if you like. You can get to know him. I'm sure you two would get on.'

'I'd love to, but not now. Enjoy being together. We'll meet up for a coffee after he's gone. You can tell me all about him then, OK?'

'What are you doing this weekend, if our outing isn't on any more?'

'I'll go home. I haven't seen Mum and Dad for ages and Mum has started nagging,' Kate replied.

'OK. We'll chat soon.'

'Yes, bye, Gail. Enjoy yourself.'

'I will.'

Kate had time to think about James, and about Alex, and was glad she knew with certainty now that neither of them were right for her. She'd done the right thing and not tried to cling on to misleading and broken dreams.

Kate walked past Chris's shop on her way to the bank and couldn't resist looking in, but he wasn't in sight. She went in and chatted with Carole.

'Where's Chris?' she queried after asking about Carole's family.

She wanted to put things right between them again if she could. She didn't intend to bring up the subject of Alex, though, because Chris had told her plainly enough that she shouldn't come complaining to him.

'He's gone to meet a producer who's making a period film in a rented manor

house in the middle of Wales somewhere. Completely off the beaten track
apparently. The producer wanted Chris
to see the place so that he can get into
the atmosphere. Chris wanted to check
if the local historical society has any
information regarding clothes of that
particular era.'

Kate nodded.

'Seems a bit over the top to me. He
doesn't normally have to know the background setting, does he? I know that he
often asks what the scene is about, so
that the costume is spot on, but that's
about as far as it goes generally, isn't it?'

Carole shrugged.

'You never know what producers or
directors will demand. Chris has worked
with this producer before. He thinks that
when Chris sees the house, he'll produce stuff that fits the film down to a T.'

'When is he due back?'

'I think he said Sunday.'

'I'll pop in at the beginning of next
week. Will you tell him I called in?'

'Of course.'

*　*　*

The weekend at home with her parents was good, even though it rained cats and dogs most of the time. Kate's mother spoiled her with her favourite food, and the weather cleared long enough on Saturday afternoon for her to go to a cricket match with her father.

She still didn't understand the rules of cricket, but it was great to sit in a deckchair, enjoy the sunshine, and only be disturbed to fetch a cup of tea for her father at the right moment.

*　*　*

Monday was her day off, so Kate slept later than usual and looked forward to mundane tasks and perhaps a little shopping.

The telephone rang just as she'd finished dressing. It was Carole and she sounded distressed.

'Kate, I'm sorry to bother you, but I didn't know who else to contact.'

'What's the matter?'

'Chris hasn't turned up for work this morning and it is very unlike him. If something delays him, he always gets in touch. He hasn't messaged to say something had delayed his departure from Wales and I'm starting to worry.

'I've tried his phone. It rings but he won't answer. I just rang his flat and there was no answer there, either. It's not like Chris.'

'Perhaps his mobile isn't working properly, and he's on his way,' Kate suggested.

'Chris would have noticed something is wrong. I usually acknowledge that I've received his message. Anyway he could phone from a petrol station or somewhere else if there was a problem with his phone. He knows that I'd wonder what was wrong. Could you go round to his flat and check if he's there? Then I know that possibility is covered. I know that you have a key. His parents have one, too, but I don't want to worry them unnecessarily.'

'Of course I can. It's no problem. I'll go right now and let you know. Stop worrying. There's a perfectly simple solution, I'm sure.'

Even though she tried to reassure Carole, strange and disquieting thoughts began to race through her mind. If Chris had promised to keep Carole informed, he'd stick to it.

Kate grabbed his flat key from the drawer and set off for the other end of the town. He had a spacious flat on the top floor of an old Victorian mansion. He'd furnished it with wonderful pieces of modern furniture, and an occasional expensive antique. Some colourful modern pictures made it a place Kate enjoyed visiting.

She ran upstairs and knocked several times before she inserted the key. She wondered if Chris did have a visitor and had lost all track of time. She hoped she wouldn't find him with a girlfriend. That idea dismayed her a great deal.

Once inside the hall, she called out loudly.

'Chris? It's me! Carole is worried because she hasn't heard from you and she asked me to check.'

There was no answer. It was silent everywhere.

Kate went into the living-room. It was tidy and morning sunshine flooded across the honey coloured floor. It was empty.

A brief look into the kitchen and the guest room produced the same result. She went towards his bedroom.

'Chris?' Calling loudly, she knocked and opened the door.

His bed was unslept in, but there was an overnight case on one chair and some clothes thrown over another. She went towards the bathroom, wondering if he was in the shower and hadn't heard her. She knocked loudly again and pushed the door open. He was in pyjamas and sprawled out on the floor.

Her heart stopped beating for a moment. Climbing over his inert body, she felt for his pulse on his throat under one ear. She didn't know if she was testing in the right position, but she could feel a very weak pulse.

His eyes were closed, and when she touched his forehead it was burning hot and covered in a thin layer of sweat. She stared in disbelief for a second until she realised it was up to her.

Talking desperately to him and trying to sound calm, she hoped he would react but nothing happened. His hands were ice-cold. Her hands began to shake as she considered his silent figure. How long had he been lying there? What was wrong with him?

A cold knot formed in her stomach. For a moment she thought she might end up in a collapsed heap next to him, but she pulled herself together. He was unconscious and not responding. Scrabbling in her pocket, she found her mobile and called for an ambulance.

She fetched a pillow and grabbed the duvet from his bed to cover him, tucking it in on the sides. There was no visible injury, but he was too heavy for her to move from the tiled floor. She knelt at his side and kept talking. She wasn't aware of what she said — she just wanted him to sense someone was with him.

It seemed an eternity until the doorbell announced the arrival of the ambulance men. She followed them to the bathroom and stood in the doorway, clenching her hands so tightly her nails bit into her palms.

They examined him quickly.

'He needs immediate hospital care,' one of the men announced. 'He has an abnormally high temperature. He doesn't seem to have any head injuries, or injuries of any other kind. It looks as though he just collapsed. His heart seems to be OK, but it needs checking properly, and we need to find out what caused him to collapse. I don't like the sound of his lungs.'

They asked questions Kate couldn't answer. How long he'd been lying there; if he'd recently been ill; if he'd had contact with anyone with a contagious disease, or if he was allergic to penicillin.

'I found him like that and phoned you minutes later, I don't think he's been ill. I saw him about a week ago and he was fine. I don't know about a contagious disease. He was away for a couple of days in Wales. I think he came back yesterday, but I'm not sure.'

'Are you related, miss?'

She shook her head.

'Girlfriend, perhaps?'

'No. I'm a friend.'

The man nodded reassuringly.

'Well, we'll get him to hospital. They'll soon find out what the problem is.'

As they prepared to put him on a stretcher, the realisation of it all sent terror through her and all colour drained from her face. She couldn't lose Chris. It was a possibility that had never occurred to her before. She had never realised until this moment just how important he was to her.

'Can I come with him to the hospital?' she asked, trying to speak calmly. 'I'll contact his parents from there.'

They nodded.

'That would be a good idea.'

They lifted Chris on to the stretcher and strapped him in. He was ghostly pale and there was still no reaction. Kate longed to reach out and stroke his face.

'It's a good thing you came along when you did, miss. Who knows what would have happened otherwise.'

She still felt unable to absorb what had happened. Terrible regrets assailed her when she remembered how they'd parted that day she went to London to meet Alex.

She locked the door and followed the paramedics as they loaded him into the ambulance.

★　★　★

At the hospital, his stretcher disappeared into the emergency treatment room. She pulled herself together and went back to the reception area. She rang enquiries, and asked for his parents' telephone number.

They no longer lived in the town. When his dad had retired, they'd sold the house and moved to a smaller bungalow in a nearby village. She'd known them as long as she'd known Chris.

His mother picked up the phone, and after expressing preliminary pleasure when she heard it was Kate, there was a prolonged silence when Kate began to explain what had happened, and where Chris was.

'We'll come immediately, Kate.' His mother's voice shook. 'They don't know what's wrong?'

'Not at the moment.' Kate tried to reassure her. 'He's in good hands and I'm sure they are doing their best to find out what caused it all.'

'You'll stay there?'

'Of course. I'll be here when you arrive. Try not to worry too much.'

Kate sat down on a chair in an alcove, overlooking the arrival area. Then she remembered Carole. She must be wondering what had happened.

Kate rang her and explained.

Carole was shocked.

'I knew something was wrong. He always keeps me informed of where he is during business hours in case a customer calls. I pray it's nothing serious. He had a bad cough at the end of last week and I told him to go to the doctor, but you know what men are like.'

'Did he? It was lucky that you phoned me and asked me to check on him. If I hadn't gone there . . . '

'It doesn't bear thinking about, does it? You'll let me know as soon as you have more information?'

'Yes. I just contacted his parents, and they are on their way. I don't suppose that the medical staff will give me any information as I'm not related. I'll phone you and keep you in the picture.'

'If I can do anything to help, just let me know. Tell that to his parents, too,' Carole said.

'I will. Thanks, Carole.'

Kate slumped into the chair and felt useless.

Time dragged and she checked her

watch by the minute. Surely someone must know what was wrong by now?

Half an hour later, she was relieved to see Chris's parents hurrying towards the entrance. After quick hugs, they went off to look for someone who could supply more information.

Time dragged again until his dad came back to her.

'They have just got the results of the X-rays. He's suffering from severe pneumonia. They're pumping him full of antibiotics and oxygen.

'They're going to keep him under observation until he regains consciousness. They are fairly optimistic that they've caught it in time, but it depends on how he reacts to the medication.'

Kate's voice faltered.

'But it's not life threatening, is it?'

He shrugged and his eyes were misty.

'They mentioned intensive care, but that depends how he reacts to the initial treatment. We have to wait and hope. Thank God you found him, love.'

He hugged her tightly and she had to

keep her tears in check.

'Why don't you go home?' Chris's dad suggested. 'There's no point in you sitting here waiting. As soon as there's any change, I'll let you know.'

She pulled herself together.

'Yes. You will phone?'

'Of course. I'll ring, I promise.'

She smiled and nodded.

'I'll be waiting.'

He turned and left her staring after him as he disappeared down the corridor.

★ ★ ★

Kate busied herself when she got back to the flat. She wasn't aware of what she did, but she had to keep herself occupied.

She phoned her mother that evening and told her what had happened.

'Chris? You two were always together like Laurel and Hardy. He spent so much time here, listening to records and doing homework with you. We always liked him. He had a mischievous look about him sometimes, but he never overstepped the mark. He still calls in for a few minutes if he is in the area.'

'Does he? I didn't know that.'

'Give him our love when you see him. Pneumonia isn't as serious an illness as it used to be, although it depends on all sorts of things. Don't worry too much. He's in the right place. Have you heard if he's making progress?'

'No, they promised to call as soon as there was any change.'

'There you are, then. Get something to eat and try to think of something else.'

On the brink of tears again, she managed a tremulous reply.

'I can't, that's the trouble. Bye, Mum. I'll let you know.'

'Bye, love.'

Kate knew she wouldn't be able to eat. She went for a walk with her phone in her pocket.

The streets were empty except for

occasional people out with their dogs. The main street was almost as empty but flooded with light from the shop windows.

She wandered up as far as Chris's shop and thought how much he'd achieved by sheer hard work and knowledge. She thought about the millions of moments she'd shared with him.

By comparison, the illusions she'd had about Alex or James faded to become meaningless. There was no other man who could ever compete with Chris. He was good, with a good heart, and he'd always been there for her, no matter what.

After a sleepless night, she was getting out of the shower when her phone rang. She grabbed it and recognised his dad's voice.

'He's out of the woods, love. The antibiotics are working well. He woke up for a minute or two and registered that we were there. His mum is so relieved, and I am, too, of course.'

Kate felt a warm glow flow through

her. She smiled broadly.

'That's wonderful. I'm so glad.'

'The hospital suggested that we go home for a couple of hours and get some rest. They said he is off the danger list, and they told us sleep is the best thing for him at present, and if he continues to make progress he may be fit enough to talk to us when we come back later on.'

'Should someone be with him? I'll go if you like.'

'No, that's not necessary. I don't think they'll let anyone else in until he is a lot stronger, but I'm sure he'll want to see you as soon as he's feeling better.'

'As long as he is getting better, that's all that matters. Thanks for ringing. Give him my love if he's awake this afternoon, and my parents send theirs, too.'

Is It Love?

Chris recovered more quickly than even the hospital expected, and three days later there was talk about discharging him.

His mum rang Kate on the second day after his admittance.

'Chris wants to see you. He's feeling much better and they're allowing visitors, as long as there aren't too many and they don't stay too long. Why don't you pop in tomorrow afternoon if you have time?'

'I will,' Kate replied, feeling elated. 'I'll take a late lunch break, and I promise not to tire him.'

'He's still worn out, though he won't admit it. We never stay long, either. He's saying he wants to go home. I tried to persuade him that when they discharge him he should come to us for a while, but he won't hear of it. He says that as soon as he gets out, he wants to go back to his flat.'

Kate laughed softly.

'Knowing Chris, he won't want fuss. As long as he realises he has to rest until he feels fit again.

'He'll hate being out of action for a while, but I'm sure Carole will cope with the business until he's fully recovered. If we stock up his fridge, he'll be OK and you can keep a distant eye on him.'

'Yes, you're right. Chris doesn't like being mollycoddled. He never has.'

'Does he need anything?' Kate asked. 'Fruit, magazines, books?'

'Don't worry about taking him anything. He can't be bothered at the moment.'

★　★　★

Chris was lying quietly in his hospital bed and was still very pale. His hair was untidy and sticking out in the wrong places.

When Kate reached him, his prominent cheekbones seemed more noticeable, and his eyes were closed.

She had bought a bunch of Michaelmas daisies on the way, and backed out again to ask where she could find a vase.

She arranged the flowers and sat down quietly by the bedside.

Chris must have sensed someone was there. His eyes opened and he gave her a weak smile.

'Ah! My guardian angel.'

She smiled.

'You gave us quite a shock.'

His eyes were too large in his face. Kate had never seen him look so vulnerable.

'From what my parents tell me, you found me in the bathroom and started the ball rolling.'

She nodded.

'Actually, Carole was your guardian angel. She was worried about you because you hadn't been in touch and she knew I had a key. I've never been more shocked than when I found you on the floor.

226

Can you remember what happened? She told me you had a bad cough and wouldn't go to the doctor.'

'That's true, but they tell me that wasn't the reason. It's a virus infection. Perhaps it developed faster because I wasn't feeling fit at the time, but it would have developed anyway. I didn't notice that it was anything unusual. I presumed it was just the start of the flu.'

'And you can't remember collapsing in a heap?'

There was amusement in his eyes.

'No! It's never happened to me before. I'd just decided that sweats, shivers, and headaches meant I had to get dressed and go to the doctor.

'It rained all the time I was in Wales and I thought the cough had developed into something more annoying. As you know, I didn't make it to the shower, or to the doctor, either.'

'You made it here instead. This place is full of doctors and some very attractive nurses, too.'

His mouth twitched with amusement.

'Yes, I've already noticed that — the attractive nurses bit.' He saw the flowers. 'For me?'

'Is there anyone else I should supply with flowers in this ward?' He clearly enjoyed her bantering and Kate was glad he sounded OK.

He was silent for a moment.

'Do you know there is some kind of Chinese saying that if you save someone's life you are responsible for them for ever?'

She had a lump in her throat.

'Is there? Then I'll have to grin and bear it, won't I?'

He surprised her by changing the direction of the conversation.

'I'm sorry — about the atmosphere and the way we parted when you were going to London. It was all none of my business.'

'I'm sorry, too. We don't usually get so uptight with each other, do we?'

'Was it a successful trip?'

'For Gerald, yes; for me, no.'

He nodded but asked no more questions.

'I'll tell you about it when you're feeling better.' She changed the subject. 'I hear there are hopes of your discharge?'

He studied her face.

'Yes. I feel much better every single day. They keep telling me to go to sleep, but they get me up now and then to get the circulation going. If things are OK, they'll let me go home in a day or two.'

'You don't want to go home to your mum?'

His eyes widened.

'Heaven forbid. She'll try to spoon feed me chicken broth every day and never let me out of her sight.'

'But if you go back to your flat, you must take it easy for a while. If you overdo things you'll be back at square one.'

'I know that. My favourite nurse has been lecturing me. Lots to drink, light meals, plenty of rest, no unnecessary exertions, and regular check-ups with my local GP for a while. Will you come to visit me?'

She shrugged to hide her confusion.

'Only if you swear to behave.'

'Cross my heart and hope to die.'

They looked at each other when his words were out and both of them began to laugh.

Perplexing emotions began to race through Kate's mind. The situation between them had changed and Kate wasn't sure that she could hide her nervousness when she was so close to him.

Would he notice one day and ask why? Could she bluff and pretend?

She was almost relieved when she saw his parents. She stood up.

'Your mum and dad are here. I'm delighted that you're feeling better. I'll come and visit you when you're back in your flat.' She bent down and kissed his forehead.

'You do that. I'll be waiting.'

Kate smiled and greeted his parents,

then she left them, turning at the door to look back.

Chris was still watching her and he lifted his hand.

Her feelings confused and bewildered her, but her heart sang because he was on the way to recovery.

Slowly she could begin to finally admit that she loved him. She had a few days to practice self-control and of keeping her emotions in check.

When his mother rang to tell Kate that Chris was being discharged, Kate left it up to his mother to prepare his flat for his return and stock his fridge.

The doctors were sure that if he followed their advice, it was simply a matter of time before he would be completely recovered.

It was enough for Kate to know he was getting better.

A Dream Come True

One evening the following week the phone rang. Kate wasn't expecting to hear Chris's voice so she was caught off guard.

'Kate? It's me.'

She pulled herself together.

'Chris!'

'You promised to visit me. I've waited in vain.'

'I didn't want to come too soon,' she replied, flustered. 'Of course I want to see you, but you are supposed to be recovering and keeping quiet.'

'Rubbish! I am behaving and I want to see you. Come round — now, if you have nothing else planned.'

'OK, I will . . . if you're sure?'

'Please. Save your compassion. My mother fusses all the time. I love Mum, but I'm glad to see her close the door when she goes. She makes me feel like a five-year-old.'

'Does she bring you chicken broth?'

He chuckled.

'Every day.'

'Come, Kate, and help shatter my boredom.'

She grabbed her coat and keys and set off. She wanted to see him, perhaps more than he wanted to see her, and she hoped she could keep up the pretence long enough.

He opened the door immediately. He must have been waiting.

He looked better. A little thinner perhaps, and his skin had lost some of its slight tan, but his eyes twinkled in amusement as he held the door open and ushered her in.

They wrapped their arms around each other in silent greeting and kissed each other's cheek.

He studied her face with an enigmatic gaze for an extra second. The sensation of their entwined bodies was too close for comfort and Kate was afraid of revealing all there and then. It felt heavenly and Kate secretly memorised the moment for later, when she was alone and out of danger.

The relief when they parted was short-lived because she still felt ill equipped to cope with the way her mind and body were reacting.

She reminded herself she only intended to stay for a short time, and this was the beginning of finding out how to cope with being with him without him realising just how much she loved him.

She couldn't imagine a life without Chris. She realised now that he had always been the special someone she hoped to find one day. They had always taken each other for granted and she had never stepped back and asked herself why he was special, until she nearly lost him for ever.

If she told him now that she loved him, he would feel sorry for her, then embarrassed, and finally it would be the end of their friendship.

With his arm draped casually round her shoulder, they drifted down the hallway and went into the living-room. The lights were low, the room was warm and comfortable, and some soft music played in the background.

When his arm fell away, she recovered slightly.

'I like this room,' she commented.

'There's lots of light, and I like the way you've mixed modern and more antiquated aspects. I love your paintings, too.'

'You've told me that before,' he said smoothly. 'Are you after my paintings? You can't have them. I like them too much myself. You were the one who persuaded me to buy some antiques in the first place. Perhaps that's why you like visiting me? Are you only after my possessions?'

She made a face and tried to sound dispassionate.

'Don't be daft! You know what I mean. As soon as you had a bit of spare money, you went for quality, and that pays off. My flat is a mess in comparison to yours because I started out with items that no-one else wanted, and have never had the money to create the kind of home I want.'

He stuck his hands in the pockets of his jeans.

'You helped me choose most of this stuff, remember? If you earned more you would eventually end up with perfect surroundings. I like your flat. It's comfortable, cosy and has a good colour scheme. Stop griping!'

Her sense of humour took over.

'You're only being kind and flattering.'

'I'm not. I told you before that I never try to flatter anyone. I've discovered it's too stressful. What would you like to drink? I'm not supposed to drink alcohol, but don't let that stop you.'

'White wine if you have some.'

He poured her a glass and sat down on the couch next to Kate.

She was careful not to touch his fingers when she took the glass.

He laid an arm along the couch.

'So, tell me some news. News of the outside world. Carole refuses to tell me exactly what is going on at the shop, apart from saying things are fine and I should keep my nose out of things for a while. My mother relates what my father is doing in the garden every time she comes, and various other mind-boggling information, like Aunt Barbara's sciatica is getting worse. Friends phone, but they're afraid they'll exhaust me, so they promise to come later. I even had to persuade my best friend to call in. Why?'

She straightened and spoke in a controlled voice.

'I have the same excuse as the rest. I know you need peace and quiet — doctor's orders. I don't intend to stay long, either.'

He ran his hands through his hair and it sprang back into position.

'Rubbish! Too much peace and quiet is bad for me. I can't read books twenty-four hours a day. Admittedly I do nap more than usual now and then, but apparently that is quite normal.'

She nodded.

'I think you know the doctors warned

you that you'll feel tired and unwell for a while yet. Are you eating properly?'

'My mother is watching my fridge like a hawk. Don't you start, too! Next time you come please bring me a pizza.'

'I will, if that's what you want. You're not on a diet.'

He crossed his legs and leaned back into the leather sofa.

'So what happened in London? Not the bit about the evaluation of the painting — tell me about the rest.'

'I hate to admit it, but you were right. I'm sure that Alex liked me, and I like him, but not in the same way. Friendship was enough for me, but not for him. I didn't really reckon with that, although I should have picked up on the signals because we were different in many ways, but he kept trying to keep the connection going. He believed I would come round to his way of thinking eventually.

'He didn't even ignore the subject of Claire — his girlfriend. I think he imagined he could either patch things up with her, and keep me in reserve, or drop her completely and tempt me with travelling the world with him if that went wrong. He always seemed so genuine, so nice and ordinary. I didn't think he'd have hare-brained schemes that included me. I realise now that I didn't know him properly. I made up my own picture of what he was like.'

Chris leaned forward and his hands dropped between his knees.

'And was that knowledge devastating?'

'No, it wasn't. I even wondered if it was my fault — if I'd given him the wrong kind of signals.'

'No regrets?'

She took a sip of the wine and met his glance.

'No, none at all. I now think that if I felt anything at all, it was just hero worship. He was an unusual man with a colourful, exotic background, and that blinded me a bit.'

He reached forward and took her free hand.

'I'm glad. You are much too good for him, and I say that without knowing him myself.'

Kate's heart jolted and her pulse pounded. She saw a new expression, a kind of flame in his eyes, and it startled her for a moment.

'Actually, I was beginning to wonder how many new romances I could put up with,' he added.

Her mind was a crazy mixture of hope and fear, and the effect of him holding her hand gave her a warm glow.

She admitted how much she loved the comfort of his nearness. Seeing him now so close, she couldn't understand why she had never realised that Chris was the only man she had ever really loved, or ever would. There had always been an indefinable bond between them.

She looked at him and wondered if she was mistaken when she noticed a flicker of interest mixed with apprehension in his expression.

'I grew up naturally expecting there would be another central man in your life one day,' he began. 'I'm not talking about the occasional dates when you were still a teenager. I mean someone like James. I suddenly realised there was a real danger I would lose you when he took over the central position in your life, and I didn't like that at all.'

Kate cleared her throat and wondered where this conversation was heading. At least he didn't like the idea of her relationship with James.

'James? You were worried about James?'

He nodded.

'I was never happier than the day when you dumped him. No sooner had I decided I had to make my own move, you started bringing Alex regularly into our chats. I didn't know how to react to that. I looked him up on the internet and wondered if he might blind you with charisma, if he wanted you as I did.'

He got up, took the glass from her hand and dropped down beside her.

'I hope I'm not doing the wrong

thing here. I can't carry on pretending, because I've come to a crossroads in my life. I will be ending the best friendship I've ever had if I get things wrong now.

'Since my stay in hospital, I've realised I have to tell you how I really feel about you,' he went on. 'I don't want to be just your friend, Kate. I want you to belong to me. I'm not telling you because you've rejected the possibility of Alex. I would have got up the courage to tell you anyway, no matter what happened.

'I've loved you maybe from the day we met, but I knew it with certainty when I realised I could lose you for ever. It took all my determination not to interfere too much. I wanted you to be happy.'

Her heart was hammering foolishly and her stomach churned. Colour flooded her cheeks.

It felt a little strange to talk with him of his love, but he was giving her the chance to be truthful, too.

She gave him a tentative smile.

'I have a confession to make, too. I

was devastated when I found you on the bathroom floor. I think I've always loved you, but until that moment I'd never faced what I might actually lose. It made me realise the difference between the pretended love I felt for James, and the real love I feel for you. I love you, Chris, I always will. I don't know why I was so blind for so long, but I'm not any more.'

Happiness lit his face. His hands cradled her face and his lips covered her mouth. She was almost shocked at her own eager response and she locked herself into his embrace.

Kate had never felt such an overwhelming reaction before. His kiss sent tingles through her.

She curled into the curve of his body.

'Hey! You are supposed to be resting and recovering,' she pointed out.

He threw back his head and laughed.

'This is the best thing that's ever happened to me. I have the feeling that I have waited most of my life for this moment. I'm not tired. I'm just mad that we have both wasted so much time.'

Kate was certain that he loved her as much as she loved him. She shook her head.

'No, I don't think we have wasted it in the way you mean. This is the right moment for us both. You said you worried about James and I always felt jealous whenever you mentioned girl-friends, but neither of us realised why we felt that way. Now we do. This is the perfect moment for us both.'

His breath was hot against her ear as he whispered, 'Remind me to thank those rather stupid men one day! They had the chance to persuade a fantastic woman to love them and they wasted their chance.'

He pulled her closer and held her tight.

*   *   *

Early the next morning, Chris called at Kate's flat to walk with her to the Treasure Trove.

It was a beautiful morning. The birds were chirping in the undergrowth, there wasn't a cloud in the sky, and the air was clear.

Kate decided that the whole world must notice that she glowed with happiness.

When she answered the door, she pretended to be angry.

'You promised to rest! It was so late when I left last night!'

He chuckled.

'I didn't want you to leave. I couldn't sleep afterwards anyway. I won't let you leave so easily from now on.'

She laughed.

'I couldn't sleep, either,' she admitted. 'It was better that I did leave. I'm still scared that you could suffer a relapse.'

'Stop fussing. Fresh air is doing me the world of good, and knowing we are together will make all the difference.' He kissed her.

His expression told her how he gloried in their shared moments.

'I can't believe it,' he told her,

smiling. 'You're mine. It's a dream come true.'

She felt a wave of pleasure.

'Can you imagine how our parents will react?'

He chuckled.

'I can imagine they'll be delighted. Perhaps they even hoped we'd end up together one day. They know we've definitely stood the test of time.'

They strolled the empty streets, their arms entwined. He went inside with her when they reached the Treasure Trove. They had found their haven at last.

When Gerald arrived, they noticed him, but went on kissing as if nothing mattered any more. They were free to admit to themselves and others that they had waited far too long to realise they belonged together. They were at one, content that anyone, even Gerald, could see them.

Gerald smiled and his cheeks bulged like pink apples as his smile broadened. Kate had chosen someone decent at last.

He liked the boy, always had. Chris would care for her, and Gerald wouldn't need to worry about finding a replacement.

One day Kate could take over the antiques shop. Elaine had suggested it months ago, as they had no children who would inherit. Kate would most likely make a bigger success out of it than he had.

'Any chance of a cup of tea, or am I interrupting something and expecting too much of my employee?' Gerald teased. 'Haven't you anything better to do, Chris?'

Chris shook his head.

'No, I haven't. You'll have to get used to it, Gerald. Kate's my girl.'

Books by Wendy Kremer
in the Linford Romance Library:

REAP THE WHIRLWIND
AT THE END OF THE RAINBOW
WHERE THE BLUEBELLS GROW WILD
WHEN WORDS GET IN THE WAY
COTTAGE IN THE COUNTRY
WAITING FOR A STAR TO FALL
SWINGS AND ROUNDABOUTS
KNAVE OF DIAMONDS
SPADES AND HEARTS
TAKING STEPS
I'LL BE WAITING
HEARTS AND CRAFTS
THE HEART SHALL CHOOSE
THE HOUSE OF RODRIGUEZ
WILD FRANGIPANI
TRUE COLOURS
A SUMMER IN TUSCANY
LOST AND FOUND
TOO GOOD TO BE TRUE
UNEASY ALLIANCE
IN PERFECT HARMONY
THE INHERITANCE
DISCOVERING LOVE

IT'S NEVER TOO LATE
THE MOST WONDERFUL TIME
OF THE YEAR
THE SILVER LINING
THE POTTERY PROJECT
SOMETHING'S BREWING

We do hope that you have enjoyed reading this large print book.

Did you know that all of our titles are available for purchase?

We publish a wide range of high quality large print books including:
Romances, Mysteries, Classics
General Fiction
Non Fiction and Westerns

Special interest titles available in large print are:
The Little Oxford Dictionary
Music Book, Song Book
Hymn Book, Service Book

Also available from us courtesy of Oxford University Press:
Young Readers' Dictionary
(large print edition)
Young Readers' Thesaurus
(large print edition)

For further information or a free brochure, please contact us at:
Ulverscroft Large Print Books Ltd.,
The Green, Bradgate Road, Anstey,
Leicester, LE7 7FU, England.
Tel: (00 44) **0116 236 4325**
Fax: (00 44) **0116 234 0205**